it was always
her

J. L. Witterick

IT WAS ALWAYS HER

Cover Graphic Artist: Philip Estrada
Cover Model: Vivian Vo-Farmer

iUniverse books may be ordered through booksellers or by contacting:

iUniverse
1663 Liberty Drive
Bloomington, IN 47403
www.iuniverse.com
844-349-9409

ISBN: 978-1-5320-6560-6 (sc)
ISBN: 978-1-5320-6561-3 (e)

Library of Congress Control Number: 2019900635

Printed in the United States of America.

iUniverse rev. date: 09/03/2021

To my parents who left their homeland in
search of a better life for their children.
Everything good that has come my way was
made possible by this act of courage.

Thank you Mom and Dad.
I love you forever.

What am I living for and what am I dying for are the same question.
—Margaret Atwood

Tom Waites

One

"Rachel!" I cry out with every breath of my being. But it is too late. The bullet has pierced her heart, unfurling a burst of red in every direction, and she falls, falls, falls in slow motion.

The movement is melodic, like the graceful stroke of an artist's brush—her head tilts backward, her eyes close in submission, her hair floats freely—until suddenly, it all halts with a sickening thud as her body strikes the ground.

Blood seeps from her lips, runs down her arm, gathers at her bracelet. She lies broken, twisted, shattered...her white dress crumpled and marred.

Jolted awake, I open my eyes and realize

I am still in bed—drenched in sweat and paralyzed with fear.

Each night, it is the same.

Each night, I watch her die.

Two

In the history of the world, there have been three wars that reached every corner of the earth. They started in 1914, 1939, and now 2025. A massive loss of life was the result of the first two, but we recovered. Will it be the same again? Will we rebuild when it is over?

Hard to say.

Our weapons are unprecedented.

I have known this war was coming for forty years. Watching it unfold was excruciating—like letting people board a plane that was doomed to crash. This time I know what to do. This time I will save her, and she will save us all.

On a clear day, the Statue of Liberty can be seen from miles away. For over a century, she has stood for freedom, democracy, and justice. When immigrants first passed through the ports of New York, they would look up at her and be assured that they had arrived in the promised land.

This morning, a deafening blast was heard on Liberty Island. In a cloud of dust, the statue was left standing without her arm holding the torch—the torch with a gold-plated flame to shine brightly—the torch that symbolizes light over darkness, hope over fear. Destroy a symbol and you destroy all that it represents. The enemy has struck at the heart of America.

How did it go so wrong?

How did we end up here?

Looking back, it started out innocently enough. The emergence of a coronavirus, similar to the common cold, is a concern at first but not a game changer in anyone's mind.

This disease, however, spreads like wildfire and proves to be far more lethal than anyone ever imagined. It takes less than a year for millions of people to lose their lives. A global pandemic, not seen in a hundred years, is declared.

Countries shut their borders and their

economies, cut down at the knees, topple over like a row of dominos. Record unemployment, social unrest, and political turmoil ensue—a formula for colossal instability.

Territorial disputes erupt around the globe. Nations, insecure about their defense capabilities, look to strength in numbers. They form strategic alliances like boys who join gangs for protection.

The end result?

A divided world.

The spark that ignites this powder keg turns out to be of all things...a drought. Without water, crop failures and food shortages are in store for two neighboring countries.

Hungry people have nothing to lose. It is the impetus for most revolutions. Irrigation would solve the problem.

Leaders from both sides send in their armies to secure a river that has, up to now, been shared peacefully. Shots are fired, casualties mount, and before the rest of the world is aware, war breaks out.

One by one, countries bound by their mutual defense treaties are drawn into the conflict...until all are immersed in battle.

History just repeated itself. The Third World War plays out exactly the same way as the previous two.

Could the president have taken action to defuse these black swan events—events that are inherently unpredictable?

No. Not likely. But, as has always been, we need to blame someone. For most, the man in charge is an obvious choice.

Twelve titans of industry, politics, and the military are among those who are desperate for change. Tonight, in the nation's capital, they have gathered to cast their votes. It is unusually cold for November in Washington, not that it matters to me. I can see and hear every nuance of their meeting from the warmth of my remote location.

These men and women, drawn from all walks of life, have nothing in common except for three things: immense wealth, political influence, and a willingness to commit murder.

Seated around an elongated table, they remind me of *The Last Supper;* and I wonder, *Which one will be the first to betray his leader?*

William Hamilton III, a distinguished gentleman in his sixties, whose ancestry dates back to the *Mayflower*, expresses his self-doubt. "President Campbell is a fine man. Truly wants the best for the country."

Rogan Stoats, a self-made billionaire, sneers at such a thought. "My mother wants the best for the country too, but that doesn't make her qualified to run it. If she were president, I'd shoot her myself."

It does not escape anyone that Rogan is the kind of person who sells you out for a dollar. If they knew that his corporation was crumbling at the foundation, they might better understand his angst.

Rogan's luxury hotels and convention centers have suffered greatly from a downturn in travel. With cash flows barely covering payroll, his prized properties, including the one facilitating this meeting, will be liquidated at a time when assets can only be cleared at rock-bottom prices.

Pounding the table with a tight fist, Rogan makes his impatience known, "This gets done now!"

William barely hides his disgust as he asks himself, *How did I end up in the same room as someone like this?*

These thoughts would have festered in his mind if a greater voice did not stamp them out. *You know why!*

William Hamilton III, with a pedigree that includes U.S. senators and governors, is fully aware of why he is here. He wants the president dead too.

The assassination of a president, never an easy task, can be distilled down to two distinct parts: kill the man and don't get caught. It is the latter that is problematic.

An entire nation will demand answers. Investigations will be unending. Someone will have to pay. Among the twelve, just one needs to cave for all to be brought down...a chain as strong as its weakest link.

But what if the murder is not that of the commander in chief? What if the murder is that of an ordinary teenager? What would the scrutiny be then?

Random, inexplicable homicides are common occurrences. At the funeral, friends and family will lament that a boy with such promise was lost. They will say he was a loving son, a good student, a promising athlete, and so forth.

Notwithstanding the sadness in his community, it will be local news and soon forgotten. There will not be outrage that the future president of the United States was just taken down—even if it is true.

Project Yesterday is perfect this way.

Kill the president in high school.

*****

Professor Nathan Lore has a reputation that precedes him. At the age of 35, he was the youngest ever to receive the Nobel prize for physics. Regarded as a genius in the scientific community, Nathan Lore stands among giants in his field. By all accounts, he should be self-confident, arrogant even. He is neither.

The professor wipes his sweaty palms against his wool pants. He clears his throat and swallows the phlegm that has come up before he speaks, "Many of you, I suspect, are skeptical about time travel. You probably think that time is constant, marching the same for everyone. Let me assure you, it is not."

Rogan grunts, annoyed to be treated like a child.

The professor continues, "Humans, by our very nature, cling to deep-rooted notions. It took us over a thousand years to accept that we live on a ball, a ball that is spinning and orbiting at the same time, even though there was ample evidence to support such a view."

The men and women in this room have a low threshold of patience. Some are tapping their fingers while others are silently screaming, *Get on with it already!*

Sensing the agitation of his audience, the professor picks up his pace, "In 1915, Albert Einstein, one of the most brilliant thinkers of the 20th century, revealed that time is an illusion. He argued that space and time are malleable in his *general theory of relativity*. Colleagues of mine have, in fact, performed experiments supporting this thesis. I have kept my work quiet—not wanting to show my hand. Today, you will see that I am light years ahead of them all."

The professor licks his lips and builds up to a crescendo, "Ladies and gentlemen, I have identified the precise location of a wormhole—a tunnel connecting spatially separated regions of time-space. Traveling through this anomaly, we can circle back to the past. It has been hypothesized but never attempted."

Around the room, eyes that were glazed over now come to life. The professor has captured the attention of his audience, and he uses this opportunity to warn of the dangers of his work.

"Wormholes are inherently unstable. They can collapse without warning. If anyone were to be passing through when this happens, he or she would be lost forever. Also, there are repercussions to tampering with the past. Events in time are sequential. Just as summer follows spring, some things cannot be changed. Imagine cutting a piece out of a water pipe and expecting the flow to continue. With so much uncertainty, I suggest we tread…"

"Thank you. That is quite sufficient," General George Emmerson, chairman of the Joint Chiefs of Staff and the top-ranking officer in the military, dismisses the professor abruptly. The general will not allow doubt to be introduced, not at this late hour.

At the onset, it was agreed that Project Yesterday would only proceed with a unanimous decision—so none could deny their concurrence and break the silence. As such, just one dissenting vote would derail his plans.

In this room are the country's elite. All the same, they fail to impress the general. As far as he is concerned, these civilians with their cushy lives have no idea of what it takes to win on the battlefield.

Big talkers. Everybody has a plan until they get punched in the face, he thinks to himself. With Project Yesterday, he would have preferred to make that decision alone.

Taking matters into his own hands is not new to the general. He has manifested his own kind of justice before. In some ways, we are alike. He is a product of his childhood...just as I am.

His father, Hank, was a bricklayer who did good work. A short temper, however, meant that Hank rarely held a job for more than a few months. At the slightest provocation, his fists would be up—ready to fight it out. His reputation meant that even managers of the busiest construction sites would think twice about bringing on such a troublemaker.

It was frustrating to Hank that no one understood or appreciated how talented he was, and he drank to dull such an injustice. Unfortunately, alcohol only magnified his nastiness. If dinner wasn't quite to his liking or if his wife looked at him the wrong way, he would be quick to teach her a lesson.

He enjoyed whipping her with his belt, and it brought him great pleasure to see her beg for mercy—knowing full well that none would be provided.

On some nights, Hank would be so drunk he would beat her using the side of the belt with the metal buckle attached. The look of terror on her face exhilarated him.

Each time, this woman—a petrified mouse in the clutches of a hawk—feared for her life. And yet, the safety of her children was her foremost concern. At the top of her lungs, she would scream for them to run and hide as the first lash descended.

The neighbors in their trailer park could hear the horrible cries, but they too were afraid of the six-foot thug with a mean streak.

Thus, for the entire summer of his twelfth year, young George mowed lawns from sunrise to sunset and saved every penny. The moment he had enough, he rode his bicycle to Walmart and purchased the Winchester hunting rifle he had seen when they went to get groceries. After that, all he had to do was wait.

It would not take long for his father to be passed out on the couch, and that would allow him to calmly put a bullet through the old man's head.

The whole thing was premeditated. Nevertheless, with a record of domestic abuse, juvenile court ruled it self-defense and George came home a hero.

Yes, the military values a man like George Emmerson: a man who gets the job done no matter how dirty, messy, or ugly that job might be.

Not for an instant has George ever regretted what he did to his father. Reinforced by the adoration of his mother and sister, he grows up believing that the *end* justifies the *means*. With such a belief, his conscience is set free.

Project Yesterday is treason of the highest order—General George Emmerson is well aware of that. Regardless, he will choose his country over his president, every time. Presidents come and go. His priority is the security of the nation.

After much deliberation, and to the satisfaction of the general, all vote in favor of the unthinkable. The members of this group, like an exhausted jury after a prolonged trial, are relieved to be done with their task. They depart, more than willing to sever their ties with each other.

The general will take it from here.

None of them—not even the general—is aware that I've had full access to this meeting and the others preceding it. A network of satellites and tracking devices keeps me well informed. Furthermore, each and every one of them has been under my surveillance for the past ten years. Their family, their friends, their secrets, I know it all.

Nothing has been left to chance.

The stakes are too high.

Three

It is a beautiful evening with a full moon hanging against a pitch-black curtain. Behind the wrought iron gates, motion sensors light the path to the stone house on the corner lot.

Leaves, dispersed by a faint breeze earlier in the day, have formed a soft blanket of fall colors. The general, deep in thought, trudges to his front door—oblivious to the autumn beauty being crushed under his footsteps.

If there is a place where he feels most at ease, it is his den: a room with solid oak panels, a wood-burning fireplace, and a desk that would take four men to move. Sitting in the corner, looking smug, is the Liberty Fatboy. This fire-resistant, 11-gauge steel safe holds 60 guns and plenty of ammunition. Anyone wanting to break into this house should think again.

Plunking down on the leather armchair that has shaped to the familiarity of his body, the general leans back and rubs his temples. His head has been throbbing all day.

By habit, he swivels right to admire his hunting trophies, mounted on the wall beside photographs of himself with past presidents. Fragments of his life in that broken-down trailer have no place here. This is his haven. This is where he is assured of his importance and superiority.

He found the meeting tiresome—and unnecessarily so. Any other outcome would have been unacceptable. "People are so dumb," he mutters to himself.

Closing his eyes, he lets the back of his neck find support naturally. It feels good to unwind. But there is much to do, and he snaps back to matters at hand as if he's just overslept on the morning of an exam.

Adjusting his posture, he places the flat of his right hand on the underside of his desk. With his identity verified, the top drawer unlocks and slides forward. He reaches in, brushes aside the 44 magnum, and retrieves a sealed envelope. Inside are photographs of young men, some in uniform.

The general peruses through his candidates, scrutinizing the information about each of them. He needs someone who can be trusted; someone who will follow orders; and, most importantly, someone who will not be missed.

He just needs one.

Bruce Meyer, a clean-cut, 18-year old boy at West Point, catches his eye. Bruce is in his first year and plays for the basketball team. He has a black belt in judo and achieved top scores on his entrance exams. West Point, an institution of discipline, will have trained him to follow orders from a commanding officer as well. So far, so good.

The general reads on.

"Next of Kin: None."

It can only mean one thing: Bruce Meyer is an orphan! No family. No questions. No loose ends.

His work is done.

Suddenly, the general winces from a sharp jab in his chest and lets go of the photograph. He fumbles for the glass bottle in his pants pocket. It's not there! In a minute, the pain will be blinding and panic, rarely felt by this man, engulfs him. He is not ready to die—not like this.

The general gropes his shirt pocket and, with relief, finds what he needs. Unscrewing the bottle cap madly, he retrieves a tablet to place under his tongue.

The absorption of nitroglycerin, the same chemical used to make explosives, is immediate. His arteries dilate just enough for blood to pass through to his heart.

Lately, these episodes have become more frequent, a reminder that time is of the essence. Eight months ago, when his condition was first diagnosed, the general took great measures to keep it hidden. If the military were aware of his health, he would be forced to step down— regardless of his rank and position. Even his wife doesn't know, but I do. It will come in handy...later.

Settled now, the general gathers the photographs on his desk, including that of Bruce, and takes them over to the fireplace. Staring at the dancing flames, he tosses the evidence to oblivion.

Mesmerized by the photos as they curl, turn to black, and disappear completely, the general ponders the possibilities of an alternate future. *Too bad I won't get credit for this,* he thinks to himself. If only he could tell his beloved mother that he single-handedly saved the world. She would be so proud.

Suddenly, the phone on his desk rings. The coincidence of such a call, at this exact moment, is unnerving. Only the president and four others in the world have access to this number, or so he thinks.

"George Emmerson?"

My voice is unfamiliar and it infuriates him.

"Who the hell is this?"

"I know about Project Yesterday," I say flatly—as if I were commenting on the weather. Nothing else is needed to capture his attention.

Four

F orbes ranks me third, at the age of 58, on its list of the world's richest people. They are right about my age. As for my net worth, they have no idea.

Secrecy is what I value above all else. On my secluded island, most of the staff are on nine-month rotations. Except for a few, none have met their boss. With the reach that my kind of money can buy, searches for me turn up blank. I literally don't exist...anywhere.

People call me neurotic, because I am rich. If I were poor, they would have called me strange.

Numerous articles have described me as aloof, brilliant, shrewd, dangerous—and depending on the source—short or tall. Some publications have gone as far as to postulate that I am the product of artificial intelligence. The only thing they know for certain is my name: Tom Waites.

I have never granted an interview to the many journalists who have written about me. If I did, this is what I would say: "True wealth is harnessed by the ability to anticipate *accurately*. Foreseeing how our world will evolve, predicting what people want even before they do, that's how you hit the mother lode."

Knowing that the internet becomes an integral part of our lives, I invest in businesses that arise from this revolution, businesses that reach to the sky and dominate all others in their class.

In 1995, I contact Jeff Bezos. He needs funding for an online shopping company and is about to borrow $250,000 from his parents. I offer it instead. We start by selling books and end up being vendors of everything under the sun. Jeff wants to call his company *Relentless*, because that is what he is. I convince him that *Amazon* would be easier to remember.

Then, in 1998, when Yahoo rejects the purchase of Google for a million dollars, I pick it up. Larry Page and Sergey Brin, the founders, are critical to the success of this company. Thus, I give these two Stanford PhD students partial ownership to remain in management. Google is so profitable that we buy YouTube and Android with cash.

Finally, in 2005, I provide venture capital to Mark Zuckerberg for a stake in his start-up: Facebook. Social media is the way to reach people when television commercials are rendered ineffective.

The most attractive businesses all have one thing in common: competitive advantage that is self-sustaining. Google, for example, gains intelligence with each search. How could a new entrant ever hope to catch up? Similarly, the sheer scale of companies like Amazon, YouTube, and Facebook make them impossible to overtake. We live in a technology-driven world, and I own it all.

Another sector where I have strategic investments is renewable energy—solar in particular. Each hour, the sun provides enough energy to satisfy the world's needs for an entire year. The problem with solar has never been the magnitude of the source. The problem has always been cost and reliability.

Mass production of solar panels solves the cost issue. It is reliability that is trickier. The sun doesn't always shine, and then there is night.

The solution?

Create batteries that can store enough energy to satisfy the needs of any household. Next, use economies of scale to drive down manufacturing costs. My factories, the size of several football fields, are designed to make these batteries affordable for everyone.

There will come a day when electricity is no longer generated by power plants and distributed via a cumbersome web of transmission lines. Houses, apartment buildings, office towers will all have solar panels on their rooftops to capture the sun's energy—energy that is stored in my batteries.

Whether the economy is strong or weak, people need to turn on the lights; they need to heat and cool their homes; and they need to cook and clean with their appliances. Providing energy is as resilient a business as you can get.

Finally, the last component of my

investments is real estate. As the saying goes, *It's the only thing they're not making more of.*

I have residential and commercial properties in San Diego, Miami, Orlando, Las Angeles, Los Vegas, Phoenix, Seattle, Austin, and Denver—the entire portfolio accumulated at distressed prices during the 2008 financial crises.

Tabloids, built on sensationalism and gossip, speculate that I have a crystal ball. More reputable sources like the *Financial Times* and *The Wall Street Journal* refuse to print such rubbish. For once, the smut papers have it right.

They do not know that I have waited—waited and planned for the last forty years—each moment not passing quickly enough. All that I am, all that I have, it is all for her. Nothing else matters.

My entire life comes down to this moment, to this inflection point. The general must be persuaded to take another course of action, but he will not see me...not unless I mention Project Yesterday.

Five

George Emmerson did not reach the pinnacle of his career, the toughest in the world, by cowering from the unknown. He will meet with me, discover how I know about Project Yesterday, and proceed with ruthless precision thereafter. A bullet is just as effective on a wealthy man as a poor one. Of that, he is certain.

The V-22 Osprey, a $70 million helicopter with the range of a turboprop airplane, is impressive at full speed. Still, it feels slow to the impatient general.

Ten soldiers, the best of the best, are prepared to kill on his command. They are seated in the back while the general is up front with the pilot. These men have not been told their destination, but being experts in navigation, they are aware of flying at low altitude over the Atlantic Ocean.

A sea of diamonds—the reflection of sunlight at a precise angle—glistens on the surface of the water. This sheet of light, moving in ebbs and flows, is breathtaking. None of them notice. They have other things on their minds.

Through the opening, where two gunners are positioned, an island with landscaped greens, sandy beaches, and a mansion perched high on the edge of a cliff comes into view. To the untrained eye, this complex could be mistaken for an exclusive luxury resort. Not so for these military experts.

They will notice the communication towers, the anti-missile artillery, and the ships circling the perimeter. The general, himself, is likely to suspect that fighter jets are on standby and submarines are on patrol. He would be correct, except that his assumptions are only the tip of the iceberg. The security on my island exceeds anything he could possibly imagine.

From a wall of screens, I observe the soldiers

speaking among themselves. Their banter is oddly amusing.

"So this is where you hold out if you've got the bucks."

"I hear he can see the future."

"I can see your future—getting your butt kicked."

"Made a fortune timing the stock market perfectly...like he knew what was going to happen."

"How come nobody knows what this guy looks like?"

"Yeah, I really want to know what he looks like."

"Your mama!"

A rebuttal, meant to be equally insulting, is silenced by the appearance of the general. These soldiers straighten their spines, throw back their shoulders, and set their sights directly ahead. Anything less would be unacceptable.

As the helicopter descends, the lawn below slides aside to reveal a landing pad. Not a word is spoken, but it's in their eyes. They are all impressed—all except the general. He is self-absorbed with purpose.

Upon touching ground, the general leaps

off. The propellers are still spinning, and he shouts to be heard, "Montalbano, Manziaris, Balfour, Gage with me. Rest of you with the chopper. If we're not back in an hour, you know what to do."

Quinn and Carson, two of my most trusted, await the general and his soldiers. My men are dressed in Hawaiian shirts and Bermuda shorts, which will be unexpected by the top military officer in the country.

Quinn offers a tray of Heinekens, chilled so that beads of sweat run down the sides of the bottles.

"Compliments of Mr. Waites."

The soldiers look on dispassionately even as their mouths water at the sight of those cold brews.

"I am not here for a drink," the general answers tersely.

Nodding with understanding, Quinn twirls the tray in the air and sends it flying.

This sudden action causes the soldiers to reach for their guns. It is only when the tray lands on a table nearby—with all the bottles standing perfectly upright—that they put away their weapons.

I staged this performance to send a message: *Do not underestimate what you see.*

It has that precise effect, because the general and his soldiers now wonder whether my men are experts in martial arts. They will never know for certain, but the answer is yes... of course.

Six

Once inside, the general and his four soldiers are shown to a room with floor-to-ceiling windows facing the ocean. They stand stone-faced, though one of them has raised his eyebrows at the stunning view.

Continuing to study the group, I notice that the general has crossed his arms and pursed his lips. His body language reveals a short fuse for being kept waiting. With such a man, who has lived by a chain of command all his life, it is imperative to establish the pecking order at the onset. Thus, I let ten minutes go by before making an appearance.

The general will see me as a threat—an obstacle to be eliminated—at least initially. For my protection, we gather in a room equipped with a supercharged magnetic field. Anything metallic: firearms, blades, explosives, and so forth, is under my control. Furthermore, an impenetrable force field keeps me safe at all times.

I offer a handshake and introduce myself, "Tom Waites."

The staunch military man in front of me has an ingrained belief system that will not allow him to understand, approve, or trust who I am. From my lean physique and the slight limp to my walk, he will judge me to be weak. Nothing could be further from the truth.

What will bother him the most will be my hair, hanging loose and touching my shoulders. The faded jeans; a linen shirt, not tucked in; and my favorite footwear, Nikes, will annoy him as well. Uniforms are irrelevant to me. I lead with innovation, knowledge, and vision— not hierarchy.

"Thank you for making the trip, George," I say as if it were a social visit.

He's on my turf now.

The general bites down on his jaw, annoyed by such a greeting. He attempts to read my facial expressions, but the mirrored lenses on my glasses only reflect back his image. If he were aware that these glasses are equipped with facial recognition capability, he would be furious.

Merely by looking at him, I have access to information about his career, his family, and his friends...assuming he has any. Furthermore, the biometric technology embedded into the frames of these glasses can analyze the residue from my handshake with him.

A slight touch to the side of these glasses is all that is required for confirmation of what I already know: the mighty general is more likely to die from a heart attack than a battle injury.

Anxious to get to business, he asks pointedly, "Why am I here?"

I reply casually, "It's best that you and I have this conversation alone."

The general grinds his teeth.

He detests casual.

I turn to the glass wall which displays a steep drop to the ocean below.

"Open Sesame."

Only part of the wall is glass. The rest is an optical illusion, cleverly engineered to deceive.

Upon my command, the entrance to another room is revealed.

"My office," I say—as though nothing were out of the ordinary.

Like a seasoned poker player, the general maintains a straight face. But there is no denying, he's a fish out of water.

"Come with me. Just you."

The chairman of the Joint Chiefs will not appreciate a direct order. Nevertheless, he will comply. Having ventured this far, what's a few more feet?

Instructing his soldiers to stand down, the general cracks his neck and follows me into the dark. We join five scientists in starched white lab coats who are observing a pool of water reminiscent of the deep blue found in the Finger Lakes.

I wave these men away and tell the general, "Look carefully."

What was water a few minutes ago has solidified and become glass-like. Images appear on the surface, one after another: children skating on an outdoor rink; a couple carrying groceries to their car; a man sipping coffee while reading the news on his iPad.

Zooming in on his tablet reveals today's date, November 27, 2025. In the background, the Statue of Liberty can be seen standing proud and *unharmed.*

On the mega LED display panel at Times Square in New York, an attractive newscaster reports: "It's looking good for Thanksgiving, folks. Lots of sunshine and warmer than usual. There's no turkey for the big guy though. Stay tuned tonight as we bring you live coverage of the turkey pardon by President Campbell."

With her closing remarks, the screen splits to show the handsome president on one side and a fat turkey on the other.

"What is this? Some kind of joke?" the general says, exasperated.

I reply with gravitas.

"Absolutely not."

His jaw hardens.

I push forward.

"There is a parallel universe to ours. We are capturing those images."

He shakes his head in disbelief.

"This is why you brought me here?"

A man who thinks in black-and-white will

reject a quantum leap of faith. Without another word, he turns his back and walks away.

I pull out my ace.

"Bruce Meyer is a good choice."

The general freezes in his tracks and swings around.

"How?"

His face is a crimson red, and he looks like he's going to burst from a uniform that fit better ten pounds ago.

"How do you know about Bruce?"

He has taken my bait.

"I know you and your, what should I call them, *partners*, blame the president for the war. There is another solution that ends better"—I pause to emphasize my next words—"for everyone."

He can hardly contain himself but manages to say, "You have my attention."

The hook is in.

"In the alternate world, the president is guided by his most trusted advisor and the outcome, as you can see, is pretty good."

"Trusted advisor? Who?" the general asks suspiciously.

"His wife."

"Katherine?"

"No, the girl he should have married."

"A girl!" the general bellows. "This is about a girl?"

He's struggling on the line and flailing about in the water. With the finesse of a master angler, I proceed to reel him in.

"Not just any girl. She is President Campbell's girlfriend in high school. If you send Bruce Meyer to save her, she will become our first lady and Project Yesterday will achieve its objective."

The general drills into me.

"Who's your informant?"

In his mind, he is trying to figure out which of the eleven betrayed him.

I scoff at his question.

"Seriously? I bought Google before the internet was understood. I positioned for online shopping before it became mainstream. Do you really think I need an informant?"

The general is on unfamiliar territory. He knows how to kill a man in his sleep, but with me, he is at a loss. His instincts, his training, his experience, they all fail him. He cannot read me, and I don't let that go to waste. Time to punch hard.

"Trust me. Your plan to eliminate the president fails. Everyone is convicted of treason, and *you*," I point out, "will be labeled a traitor."

The general stiffens—*traitor is* toxic to a man who considers himself a patriot.

"Remember *Benedict Arnold?* It will be far worse for you."

The general is well versed in history and fully comprehends my reference.

In 1780, General Benedict Arnold plotted to hand over the site of West Point to the British for £20,000 and a position as a brigadier general in the British Army. He was so detested that to this day, *Benedict Arnold* is a term used to refer to someone who is a traitor and a disgrace.

"Would be a shame to end a career that way," I say, and shifting my eyes to connect with the Medal of Honor pinned on his chest, I drive the knife deeper, "Especially one so distinguished."

He opens his mouth, reconsiders, and swallows his words. It is probably the first time he has been speechless.

I lift my wrist and speak into my watch.

"Now."

One of the scientists, who left the room earlier, returns holding a silver tray with a single envelope.

"Jack Campbell does not marry Rachel Lee, because she is killed in high school. To save her, Bruce Meyer will need these instructions."

The general does not blink.

I give his ego a calculated nudge.

"Your legacy?"

Our eyes lock—the will of two men in a silent struggle for dominance. Grudgingly, he snatches the envelope and storms out.

The quest to save Rachel, the driving force of my existence, hinges on the general siding with me. He must have absolute conviction that I can predict the future.

"I suggest you attend to your heart as soon as possible."

The chairman of the Joint Chiefs, the lynchpin to everything that matters to me, does not turn to acknowledge my remark. He has, however, glanced down at his chest. It will be fine now.

Seven

There is a room I go where I am not Tom Waites, where I do not oversee an empire, where I am but an ordinary man. After the general leaves, I seek this refuge.

My favorite place to unwind is on a well-worn sofa from the 1980s that is more comfortable than stylish. From here, I have an unobstructed view of the ocean. Next to me on the coffee table is a black-and-white photograph of a Taiwanese family.

Olena, my personal assistant for the last thirty years, serves jasmine tea. She knows it will soothe me. I stare at the waves, hurling themselves against the jagged rocks below; and I think, *Is that me?*

To be the richest man in the world—to have

anything I want at my fingertips—it makes me partly admired, mostly envied, and entirely isolated.

Olena understands my moods and leaves quietly. When she closes the door and I am alone, I remove my glasses and pick up the photograph. My fingers tremble as I trace the outline of the seven-year-old girl in the picture who is so skinny you can see the shape of her knees and ankles.

This is the girl in my dreams—the girl who haunts and sustains me at the same time. Human beings are not meant to be alone. Solitary confinement is the ultimate punishment for a reason. It breaks our spirit.

A beautiful island cannot be compared to a prison, unless you know that it is. The loneliness I feel is just as intense as if I were in a cage.

I take a sip of tea, lean back, and close my eyes...to relive the past.

Eight

Five black, bulletproof Mercedes wind along I-90 on their way to Cambridge, Massachusetts. In the back seat of the third vehicle are the most powerful man in the military and a low-level cadet. George Emmerson and Bruce Meyer have nothing in common—except for a project called Yesterday.

The general asks Bruce, "Do you know when West Point was founded?"

This is a direct question to which only a precise answer will do. Bruce tenses up. The last thing he wants is to disappoint his hero, but he cannot remember the date and guessing incorrectly would be worse.

"Sir, I am sorry to say that I do not, sir."

If Bruce were feeling inadequate before, he is even more so now.

"It was 1802," the general informs him. "The original site was a military post considered to be strategically important by George Washington."

Bruce wishes he were better versed on the history of West Point. There was just no way he could have predicted a meeting with the chairman of the Joint Chiefs of Staff!

"What is the motto of West Point, Cadet?" the general asks.

This time, Bruce is relieved to have the answer. "It is duty, honor, country, sir."

"Exactly."

The general continues with his line of questioning, "So tell me, why are you at West Point?"

"To prepare for service to my country, sir." Bruce resonates with conviction—not betraying how nervous he is to be speaking with a legend.

The general nods with approval. It is precisely what he wanted to hear, and he launches into the matter at hand.

"The war is progressing at an alarming rate. There is no choice. We have to send you back."

"Sir?" Bruce does not understand.

The general presses a button on his armrest which causes the soundproof partition to rise between the front and back seats. The soldier next to the driver is trained not to be distracted. Even so, when he hears the glass going up, it makes him wonder, *What secrets could be shared between a general and a cadet?*

The general completes his sentence, "Back in time, that is."

Bruce listens attentively, trying his best not to appear thoroughly lost.

"We think President Campbell could have prevented the war. The problem is, he needs the help of a woman who is killed before she becomes his wife."

Bruce can hardly believe what he is hearing. It is all he can do to conceal his astonishment.

"Your mission is to save her. She must survive to marry the future president." Shaking his head, the general reveals a daunting statistic, "Our casualties exceed a million, and there's no end in sight."

These pronouncements come from a man that Bruce admires. Still, how can any of it be real?

"You're the perfect age to blend in at the high school where President Campbell and his girlfriend are in their final year. You play basketball, right? I hear you're good."

"Yes, sir. Thank you, sir."

Bruce has no idea where this is going.

"Basketball was important to President Campbell. Use it to get close to him and his girlfriend—the future first lady."

At this point, Bruce feels the need to ask an obvious question. "Sir, permission to speak freely, sir?"

"Permission granted."

"What about Katherine, our first lady?"

The general dismisses that thought with annoyance, "He was never supposed to marry her." There is a gruffness to his voice, and it warns Bruce against overstepping his position again.

Inadvertently, he has prompted the general to remember his next point.

"I know your parents were in the military and killed in action. I am sorry for your loss. Nevertheless, that cannot, must not, be changed. Any deviation from the past introduces new and unknown variables. The risks are unacceptable."

With so much coming at him, Bruce needs a minute to grasp what the general is really saying. *Of course!* he realizes. *I could warn them!*

"Sir, I understand, sir. But my parents were ground troops among others."

The general huffs, *Why can't soldiers do what they are told?*

"When your parents died, you went to live in foster homes, correct?"

"Yes, sir." It was the loneliest time of his life, but Bruce has learned to mask his feelings and answers as if the question were routine.

"Your parents married against the wishes of their families, so no one came forward to take you," the general states matter-of-factly.

Bruce clenches his fists, the only hint that it still bothers him. The memory of an incident, suppressed for so many years, rises to the surface.

Dylan, a twelve-year-old bully, yanks the pillow from seven-year-old Bruce while he is sleeping. A small photograph of Bruce and his mother falls out.

Twin boys, a year younger than Bruce, wake up and gather around.

Dylan is enjoying the attention and plays it up. "Lookie here, the baby still sleeps with his mommy."

The twins know that Dylan taunts all newcomers. They should have warned Bruce. Too late now.

Bruce looks up at Dylan defiantly.

"Give it back."

The twins cringe…this won't end well.

Dylan waves the photo above Bruce's head.

"I have to tear this up. You're too old to sleep with Mommy."

The twins look on, sympathetic with Bruce but too fearful to say a word. They have, at times, incurred the wrath of Dylan themselves.

Bruce knows what he needs to do. In a flash, he grabs the knapsack from his bed and hurls it upward at Dylan, striking him like a slingshot.

Mollified by acquiescence typical of his victims, Dylan is unprepared for what is coming at him. Stunned by the painful blow, he shrieks and collapses like a rag doll, stuffed with nothing but straw.

Bruce bends down to retrieve his treasured photo, which has settled beside Dylan on the floor. Now that the excitement is over, the twins return to their bunks, sneaking an adoring look at Bruce along the way. No one notices or cares that Dylan is still whimpering.

Sitting on the edge of his bed, Bruce opens his knapsack and smiles at the three large stones inside. While the other grade two students on the field trip were collecting leaves by the riverbank, he found what would keep him safe.

Sliding the photograph back into his pillow case, Bruce falls asleep with the knapsack nearby. In the morning, they will move him to another home. No matter…he has the stones.

"Having to look out for yourself, do you think that might have shaped who you are? Would you be the same person if you had a mother who kissed that scraped knee or a father who took you camping?"

The general hammers out his next words, "I think not."

As much as Bruce wishes it were not true, the general has a point.

"You protect Rachel Lee, period."

Demanding that his soldiers be nothing but obedient, the general leans into Bruce and reiterates, "You tell no one about this. No one."

Nine

B ruce peers out from the tinted window of the Mercedes to see that they are approaching MIT, a private research university known for innovation and academic excellence. He had been curious about where they were going but did not dare to ask.

Grass left to overgrow and leaves wantonly scattered by the wind reveal that the grounds have been neglected for some time. It is survival, not aesthetics, that matters most these days. Buildings, once edifices of higher education, have been reassigned for weapons research, and they are heavily guarded.

The convoy of vehicles slows down, coming to a full stop directly in front of a newly constructed brownstone. A visual scan is performed on the immediate area before the car door is opened for the general and the cadet. Five men, heavily armed, join in before they all enter the building together.

Bruce follows without a word. He knows, *Do not speak unless spoken to.*

At the end of the hallway, they pass through a steel door so thick it might have been the opening to a bank vault. Once inside, Bruce finds himself blinking to adjust. The room, spacious and sparse, has enough lighting for a stadium.

Professor Lore scratches his head nervously, causing flakes of dandruff to fall onto his shoulders. He has been jumpy all day. Project Yesterday is the culmination of his life's work—it is irrefutable—but he needed a few more months. Adding to his stress is the fear of losing his lab should the project be delayed. No wonder deep furrows, partially obscured by horn-rimmed glasses, are entrenched on his forehead.

The professor hesitates. Should he shake the general's hand or salute him? He chooses the latter—better to err on being respectful.

General Emmerson dominates the room

with his presence. Everyone knows: the boss is here. Like a bloodhound, the general can detect the faintest scent of vulnerability. Within a matter a minutes, he has sized up the man in front of him—a lightweight with the brains of a genius.

Professor Lore is awkward at best. A restless sleep the night before, however, is not helping. Graduating from MIT when boys his age were being introduced to multiplication, Nathan Lore never developed a semblance of interpersonal skills.

He was an outcast on the first day of kindergarten, refusing to play games such as hide and seek, which he regarded as a waste of time. His parents had him tested and found that, indeed, their son was gifted.

The young boy was then accelerated through a special program with a series of teachers being his only companions. When making friends his own age proved to be awkward and unsuccessful, Nathan found it easier to devote his life to research.

People are too unpredictable, he justified to himself. And so, after the teachers departed, mathematics and science filled the void—becoming his trusted allies.

Now, after rushing through a myriad of calculations, the professor is plagued by self-doubt. A million things could go wrong! He has never been religious but silently prays for the day not to end in disaster. With feigned confidence, he tells the general, "We are ready to proceed."

A display of emotion from the general is unusual. Nevertheless, he is pleased that the project is on schedule and permits his lips to curl. History is about to change.

Bruce is taken to a curtained area, where he is given an injection which will help him acclimatize to the transport. Neatly folded on a bench nearby are clothes selected to blend in seamlessly upon arrival.

After changing, Bruce reappears in a white T-shirt, canvas pants, and a light jacket—all unbranded. On his feet are plain running shoes. Nothing to stand out.

There is much on his mind, but Bruce does not yield to curiosity. Who is he to question the highest-ranking officer in the military?

The general looks Bruce over from head to toe and hands him a thick envelope.

"Money and ID. Can't transport with too much."

"Yes, sir," Bruce replies while thinking, *Is this really happening?*

Not finished yet, the general gives Bruce another envelope, much thinner than the previous one.

"Intelligence from Mr. Waites—critical to saving the future first lady."

Bruce is about to respond when the general barks his final order, "Do not let me down, Soldier."

"Sir, yes, sir!" Bruce answers with a stiff salute.

The general has acted on his own in the redirection of Bruce's mission and, for an instant, he wonders if the best course of action might still be to terminate Jack Campbell. A sudden pang from his heart, however, reminds him of the last words from Tom Waites.

No. George Emmerson, a five-star general, will not risk everything he has done for his country to be labeled a traitor in the end. He can live with anything…except that.

Bruce slides both envelopes into his pocket, designed deeply for this purpose. Hidden inside is the photograph of his mother. The general would not approve, but how could he leave it behind?

Two men, as clinical as their lab coats, escort Bruce to a large white enclosure. Precision is vital, and they fuss with his positioning beneath the circular opening of an opaque cylinder.

Instructed to remain still, Bruce keeps his arms firmly pressed against his thighs. There is a hint of something colorful from under his left shirtsleeve. Once again, he has defied the general. Bruce tried...he really did. He just couldn't part with this keepsake.

All eyes fixate on the translucent tube as it twists down and swallows the young man below. A crisp suction sound indicates the mechanism has locked into place. Next, the white casing lowers to encapsulate Bruce completely. It is the point of no return.

The general tells himself that he made the right decision. Consulting with the others would have been tedious and a waste of time. In any case, they would never know.

Over the intercom, the professor's cautious voice can be heard.

"Subject is engaged. Transport in progress and"—he pauses— "complete."

With his business done, the general turns to leave. He and his soldiers are about to exit the building when the five Mercedes in waiting explode one after another. These multiple blasts catch the men off guard. They are, however, trained to act swiftly and pull back to the stone entranceway for cover.

Then, the entire building detonates. The general, the professor, and everyone involved with the transport have just been erased!

Seeing it unfold on my screen jolts me backward in my seat. I thought I knew about everything...but I did not see that coming.

Ten

It feels as if it were only a blink of an eye when Bruce finds himself standing alone in an open field. He looks around, bewildered.

Some of the buildings are familiar. Yet, unlike before, the lawn is meticulously manicured; squirrels wander freely in search of food; and students stroll casually to their next class. There is not a hint of war anywhere.

Bruce marvels at the serenity. *Such beauty and innocence,* he thinks to himself. His immediate task, however, is to locate Rachel Lee; and he shakes off these thoughts to quickly hail a cab.

The driver, pleased with a fare to the airport, chats it up.

"Traffic's good ahead of rush hour. Should be there in no time at all."

His ride is just being friendly, but what Bruce really wants to know is the date.

"I always forget too," the driver says. "The missus reminded me to take out the garbage before I left, so I can tell you for sure, it's Wednesday."

Bruce didn't need the full explanation.

"No, I mean what year is it?"

The driver, who had been so talkative before, is now unsure about his passenger. "It's 1985," he answers timidly. And, for the remainder of the trip, an awkward silence takes over.

When they arrive at the airport, Bruce makes his way to American Airlines. He needs a ticket to San Francisco.

The recent graduate at the counter is keen to do a good job. With a cheerful voice, she asks, "Would you like business or economy?"

"Just the cheapest seat, thanks," Bruce tells her.

"Okay. Sure thing. That'll be $115. Cash or charge?"

Having just paid for the taxi with a hundred dollar bill, Bruce knows he has plenty more in one of the envelopes.

"Cash."

From the cab driver to this girl, Bruce is struck by the affability of his encounters. It makes him wonder if people are naturally this way…when they are unafraid.

Once inside the plane, Bruce is pleased to have a window seat which works better for privacy. While the flight attendant is demonstrating routine safety procedures, he reaches into his front pocket and retrieves the two envelopes protectively.

In the first, there is a birth certificate and a passport along with the money—useful. Setting that aside, he turns his attention to the message from Tom Waites. Unexpectedly, the only thing he finds there is a blank sheet of paper!

Was the letter compromised during transport? How will he complete his mission? How will he protect Rachel Lee?

Most people would be in a panic by now. Not Bruce. For his entire life, he has confronted adversity on his own. His instincts, his ingenuity, his cleverness—all sharpened like a knife over a grindstone. Faced with this dilemma, he draws from that experience and remains calm.

DNA confirmed: Bruce Meyer
Instructions: Date activated
Read: Prom day

Bruce rubs his eyes. Where did this come from? There was nothing a minute ago! He holds the letter up to the light and scrutinizes it from all angles, looking for a clue, a hint of anything that might be helpful. Still, the only thing he sees is a plain piece of paper. What else can he do but wait?

The general had expected to preview the instructions from Tom Waites as well. To his dismay, none of his intelligence officers could decrypt the message. "We've never encountered anything like this," they told him. And, as furious as the general was about that, he had to give Bruce the letter regardless.

"Would you prefer beef or chicken?" the flight attendant asks politely.

"Beef, please."

Taken aback by such luxury, Bruce can hardly wait for his meal. Airlines in the future make their passengers pay for food and have a limited menu, like sandwiches wrapped in plastic.

After enjoying his beef tenderloin with mashed potatoes and string beans, Bruce peruses the in-flight magazine and catches some shut-eye. He wants to be well rested and alert upon arrival.

When the plane touches down in San Francisco, it is still morning. The time difference has given Bruce an extra three hours, and he moves swiftly not to waste this windfall.

In the arrivals area, he picks up a newspaper before lining up at the taxi stand. Uber doesn't exist and the smart phone hasn't been invented yet. By the time his car pulls up, Bruce has already identified several suitable locations.

His first stop is in front of a five-story apartment building that might have been respectable when it was built. The windows are covered with a thin film of dust and, on the lawn, dandelions have overtaken the grass. Rent here is low for a reason.

Bruce pays the driver, asks him to wait, and makes his way to the entrance.

Inside the narrow hallway, on the immediate left, is a handwritten sign taped to the door: "Superintendent."

Bruce knocks.

"Come on in," is shouted back at him.

As instructed, Bruce enters to find himself in a room the size of a large closet. Seated behind an aluminum desk is a man with ketchup stains on his shirt and hair that hasn't seen a comb in days.

He looks up at Bruce.

"What can I do for you?"

"You have a bachelor to rent?"

Vacancies have been higher than usual and the superintendent perks up.

"Yes, still available."

He points to a chair with a cushion that is threadbare in the corners.

"Please, have a seat."

Shoving the scattered papers on his desk to one side, the superintendent is ready for business.

"It's five hundred a month, and I need first and last up front. Minimum one-year lease. No smokers. No pets."

Just as the superintendent completes his sentence, an elderly woman with hair the color of straw and a back curved like a willow tree walks by with the assistance of a cane. She has a petite poodle on the other end of a short leash.

"Good morning, Al," she says sweetly.

"Good morning, Mrs. Goodman," he replies.

Bruce glances down at the dog and concludes that *Al* will not be enforcing any rules. No questions asked; it's perfect.

The superintendent turns his attention back to Bruce. "Wanna see it?"

Bruce counts out ten one hundred-dollar bills and lays them on the table.

"I'll take it."

Eleven

From the sidewalk, Bruce looks up to see "Abraham Lincoln High School" chiseled into the entrance arch of a mammoth stone building. *There must be over a thousand students here,* he thinks to himself. Declining enrollment will force many of these schools to close in the future. Bruce wonders if Lincoln will be one of them as he passes through its massive doors.

In the main office, two middle-aged women are engrossed in a discussion about the stores with the best sales this weekend. Through years of experience, these ladies have developed the ability to fill out forms, type letters, and perform a multitude of tasks without the slightest disruption to their conversation. One of them notices Bruce and leaves her desk to help him.

"I just moved here," Bruce tells her.

"Well then, welcome to Lincoln High."

Her warm response reminds Bruce of how friendly and trusting everyone has been.

"We just need some identification and your address and autograph on a few things," she says while retrieving several forms from under the counter. In less than ten minutes, Bruce is given a permission slip to attend class as a new student.

There is a basketball practice game in progress when Bruce enters the gym. Mr. Wyatt, the physical education teacher and coach for Lincoln's basketball team, is focused on the play and accepts the yellow slip without looking at it.

Jack Campbell receives a pass and slashes between two defenders to sink the shot in one fell swoop. Feeling triumphant, he smiles at his coach.

All at once, Bruce is reminded of a portrait that hangs prominently in Cullum Hall at West Point. In this painting, the president of the United States has the exact same expression.

"Duh! Of course!" Bruce says to himself, "What did you expect?"

Mr. Wyatt, no longer distracted, turns his attention to the new student. With half an hour left to the class, why not let the kid play? "Get changed. Extra shorts in the locker."

"Yes, sir. Thank you, sir," Bruce replies.

Mr. Wyatt is taken aback...students just don't answer that way!

Bruce does as he is told and heads straight to the change room. On the way, he can't resist another look at the future president. What a day this has been! General Emmerson and now President Campbell!

It does not take long to change into shorts, and Bruce returns swiftly. Mr. Wyatt motions Jack off the floor.

"Let's see what you got, kid."

From the get-go, Bruce is in control of the ball. He sweeps down like a gale-force wind, unstoppable until he is done with sending it through the hoop.

Jack turns to his coach.

"You thinking what I'm thinking?"

Mr. Wyatt, arms folded and eyes following Bruce, nods yes.

It is common knowledge that most basketball players are tall. Height is a natural advantage in this game. Thus, when presented with a boy who stands at five feet ten inches, the coach did not expect much.

Basketball, however, is a fast-moving game where speed, agility, and strategy are just as critical to success. In these, Bruce excels. He is a gifted athlete—no question—but there is another reason why he jumps so high and runs so fast. Three years ago, he started wearing ten-pound ankle weights. When these are removed, gravity does not hold him down like it does everyone else.

As for his height, Bruce has found a way to compensate as well. By adopting the strategies of Muggsy Bogues, Bruce can steal and pass in a way that is difficult for taller players to intercept. Muggsy was the shortest player in the history of the NBA, yet it did not hold him back. Emulating the techniques of this superb athlete is a brilliant move.

Outside of basketball, most people don't know about Muggsy Bogues and his incredible story. Raised by a single mother, he grew up in the tenements with poverty and violence for neighbors. When he was just five years old, a stray bullet shot through his arm. His father was in prison at the time. *If a guy like that can make it,* Bruce has said to himself, *so can I.*

The coach, given a player as determined and gifted as Bruce Meyer, finds himself contemplating the possibility of a state championship. *Maybe this year?*

Twelve

In 1985, with a high school cafeteria full of hamburgers, hot dogs, and french fries, it is unusual to find a boy enjoying a salad for lunch. Then again, Bruce is from a different generation—a generation that has learned to eat healthier. Fresh-grown vegetables were difficult to obtain during the war, so Bruce is savoring his meal.

Jack usually sits with his girlfriend, but today he has another agenda. Searching the cafeteria, he spots Bruce by a window and makes his way over to him.

I should really welcome the new kid, he tells himself, even though something else is on his mind.

"Impressive moves yesterday," Jack says to Bruce as he sets down his tray.

"Not bad yourself," Bruce answers. Sticking his hand out, he introduces himself, "Bruce Meyer."

A handshake? Really? Jack was not expecting such a gesture, and it throws him off. "Oh yeah, sorry. I'm Jack, Jack Campbell, captain of the basketball team."

I know who you are, Bruce thinks to himself.

From the moment that Jack saw Bruce play, he knew he had to have this talent on his team. Being too forward, however, can turn people off, so Jack keeps it light.

"Lincoln's never made it to the finals. We could use you."

"Sure. Sounds good. Thanks."

Bruce does his best to sound casual, but it is the future president! He has already been approached by the coach but doesn't mention it. Why spoil the moment?

Satisfied with the response, Jack starts on his burger and notices that Bruce is working on a salad.

"You eat like a girl!"

Bruce chuckles at the comment and continues with his lunch.

A girl with an engaging smile approaches to sit beside Jack. She has the exact same salad as Bruce on her tray. Jack looks down at her lunch and back up at Bruce. Both boys break out laughing.

"What?" Rachel doesn't understand.

"Nothing," Jack says, brushing it off.

He tells Bruce, "This is Rachel, my girlfriend."

Rachel! It's her!

Bruce sits up and takes a closer look.

Rachel has the complexion of a sun-brushed tan. Her hair is long, silky, and black. Her eyes are almond-shaped, and her mouth is delicately formed. None of her features particularly stand out, yet they come together in way that is a soft and pleasing.

"Who's this?" she asks.

Jack explains that Bruce has just moved here.

"That's great," she says before turning to Bruce. "So, where are you from?"

"Ah, New York area," Bruce replies, annoyed with himself for the awkward response. It's not as if he has never seen a pretty girl before. He can't explain it. For some reason, Rachel fascinates him. There's no logic to attraction.

She is curious to know more.

"Why'd you move here?"

Bruce blinks as if something were caught in his eye.

"My dad's company relocated."

"Oh, what's your dad do?"

"Geez, Rache. Will you cut it out already with the inquisition?"

Having just connected with Bruce, Jack doesn't want anything to jeopardize the relationship.

Rachel laughs innocently.

"Yeah, sorry about that."

She's harmless, Bruce thinks to himself. *Why would anyone want her dead?*

"You okay for practice tonight?" Jack asks. With a big game next week, it would be good for Bruce to start right away.

This invitation is precisely the opening that Bruce has been looking for, and he jumps at the opportunity.

"Count me in!"

Thirteen

The season has started out well enough. Nevertheless, Jack is anxious about their chances against Lenwood High. While seated on the bench, he whispers to Bruce, "They've got some tough players. See how the coach is fidgeting?"

Bruce had not noticed before, but Mr. Wyatt is clearly twisting his hands and twirling his thumbs.

"Does that when he's nervous. Got our butts kicked by these guys last year."

Bruce sizes up the situation and tells his new friend, "I'll send the ball to you. You know the rest." Jack nods to agree, and they knuckle punch to seal the deal.

In the game of basketball, strength in

dribbling, passing, and defense is critical to success. To win, however, a team must have players who can shoot accurately.

The ball has to go through the net to score—that's a given. Less obvious is the fact that a player who can make the outside shot forces his defender to play tight and that, in turn, creates the opportunity for a fake or breakthrough.

Is Bruce a good shooter?

Absolutely.

What's more, his skills are so far reaching that he can be effective in any position. Lincoln just gained an asset that makes it difficult—if not impossible—to beat.

The players from Lenwood have underestimated their competition. Their captain can be heard boasting, "Candy from a baby."

This is the first game for Bruce, and he is uncertain about how hard to play. Making the team at West Point was no easy task, especially for a first-year student. He knows he can make a difference. The trick will be to achieve what is needed without bringing attention to himself.

At halftime, the scoreboard shows Lenwood, the visiting team, ahead by ten points. Jack glances over at Bruce with a told-you-so look. It is the catalyst for Bruce to turn things around.

Beginning slowly, he steals the ball here and there and sends it to Jack as promised. Jack soon catches the cadence of this play and positions to score each time.

When the buzzer signals game over, Lincoln has beaten Lenwood by three points!

Ignited by this unexpected turnaround, students from Lincoln rise to their feet and cheer wildly. Four players rush in to lift Jack Campbell, the team's MVP, onto their shoulders. Cheerleaders perform a funky dance, adding to the exultation.

Rachel works her way down from the stands and waves to Jack. She can see how happy he is by the huge grin on his face. Something is bothering her, though, and she approaches Bruce.

"Why didn't you score?"

"What do you mean?"

"You made some incredible steals to get the ball to Jack. Why stop there?"

Bruce didn't think anyone noticed. Rachel is right of course. He could have made all the shots himself. Lying to her is uncomfortable, and he looks down to avoid eye contact.

"We're a team...all working together."

Rachel can see that Bruce is evading her question. Should she persist or let it go? In this moment of glory, the choice is clear.

"Okay, sure. Great game. Congrats."

Relieved to have dodged that bullet, Bruce offers her a handshake.

"Forget that!" she says while throwing her arms around him.

At West Point, many of the boys had girlfriends. Bruce always thought of them as a waste of time, a distraction. Being involved with someone could not be further from his mind. All he wants is to serve his country. But Rachel, her smile, her warmth, her laughter—there is something about her that he can't explain.

Days later, Lincoln is now the visiting team against Glencarin Collegiate. Jack and his team, full of confidence, play a strong and steady game.

The coach starts out fidgeting, but when he looks up at the scoreboard and sees how far ahead they are, he throws his hands down.

Students from Glencarin heckle and jeer each time Lincoln gains a point. It has no effect on Jack, Bruce, or any of their players. Winning feels too good.

Kora, a blond with brunette roots and enough makeup to make you wonder what she really looks like, takes the seat next to Rachel.

Everyone knows that Jack and Bruce are buddies. They also know that Rachel is Jack's girlfriend. As such, it was logical for Kora to assume that she could get what she wants by cozying up to a girl she detests.

"He's cute," Kora says, her eyes glued to Bruce's every move.

Rachel leaves that remark alone. Kora is in her English class, but they have never been friends.

"Is he seeing anyone? Does he have a girlfriend?"

Rachel doesn't answer—hoping Kora will go away.

Kora, however, is not giving up that easily. She jabs Rachel with her elbow and demands a response.

"Well, does he?"

"No, I don't think so," Rachel replies reluctantly.

"Okay then, open season!"

Kora is already plotting the best way to use this information.

Rachel stiffens and thinks to herself, *Why should I care if Kora likes Bruce?*

But I do, she realizes.

When the buzzer sounds game over, the scoreboard shows that Lincoln has defeated Glencarin by a sizable margin.

Rachel, Kora, and a handful of loyal followers punch above weight for the amount of noise they create. Jack and Bruce high-five each other while their cheerleaders launch into a flamboyant dance.

Students never interested in basketball before now stop Jack in the hallway to congratulate him. School pride swells with record attendance at both home and away games.

When Lincoln successfully advances to the semifinals, their fans go wild. "Lincoln! Lincoln! Lincoln!" they chant, creating a sound so thunderous that the bleachers reverberate like a tuning fork.

The coach beams as brightly as if he were the winner of a Powerball lottery, and the bond that was building between Jack and Bruce is further solidified.

Fourteen

To celebrate their win, Jack, Rachel, and Bruce settle on Burger Shack, a local diner where families on a tight budget can be treated to a decent meal.

"Did you see the look on his face?"

Bruce knows that Jack is referring to Mr. Wyatt and answers, "Yeah, that was sweet."

Making their coach proud is part of the reason these boys push so hard—whether they realize it or not.

"Goin' all the way!" Rachel exclaims.

Without doubt, the team is performing better with Bruce, but her conviction is based on another observation. In all the games so far, Bruce has held back until the last minute.

When they get to the finals, she is certain he will come through with what is needed.

Deep down, Jack believes they have a shot at the state championship as well. He just doesn't want to jinx it.

"Now Rache, too early for a call like that."

"Telling you right here, right now, you guys are bringing it home," she insists.

Her resolve makes Jack smile, and he puts his arm over her shoulder.

"That's my girl—the fortune-teller."

As they approach the restaurant, they see Fred, the owner, shoo away a homeless man crouched by the entrance. An old man begging for money is bad for business.

The homeless man, accustomed to being rebuked, limps across the street clutching two shopping bags stuffed with all that he owns in the world. He was coughing the night before and hunches over a water fountain to let the cool liquid soothe his throat.

Rachel pauses to look at him, while Jack enters the restaurant. Bruce, right behind Jack, hangs back to wait for her.

"Come on, Rache!" Jack calls out. His

stomach is growling, and he wants to get started on their order.

Not wanting to keep her boyfriend waiting, Rachel scurries into the restaurant with Bruce a step behind. Her mind is still on the homeless man as she wonders about how he could have ended up on the street.

Inside the restaurant, tightly-packed tables are covered with plastic tablecloths. The linoleum tiles on the floor have been worn so thin that patches of grey concrete show through in high traffic areas. Cheap paintings, the kind found in garage sales, hang lopsided on the walls with no one bothering to straighten them out. The food here must be good. People don't come for the ambiance.

A waitress, whose part-time job became a career, stops chewing her gum to ask, "What can I get ya?"

Jack turns to Bruce and Rachel.

"Three burgers and fries?"

Bruce is starving and would have said yes to anything. Rachel, on the other hand, has something else in mind.

"Could I have a veggie, please?"

"You know that's not a real burger," Jack teases.

The waitress moves on, unfazed.

"Drinks?"

"Coke for me, water for her," Jack replies.

"Water for me too," Bruce chimes in.

As the waitress walks away with their order, Jack tells Bruce, "Restaurants hate it when you ask for water. They make nothin' on that."

"Yeah, that's true," Bruce agrees.

"Rache always gets water. She thinks drinks are a waste of money. I'm pretty sure her dad had something to do with that."

"I like water," Bruce says honestly, "even if I had to pay for it." Bottled water is big business in the future.

Jack has a hard time believing anyone would spend money on what they could get for free. "People won't pay for water."

"You sure about that?" Bruce blurts out before catching himself.

With sarcasm, Jack answers, "Don't let me stop you with that groundbreaking idea."

Perrier, Evian, and Aeras all come to mind, but Bruce refrains from letting it slip a second time. He shrugs his shoulders instead to indicate, *You never know.*

The waitress brings their drinks and sets them down. "Your burgers are comin' up soon. I'll be right back."

Unexpectedly, Rachel asks for a take-out bag.

"Honey, you haven't even started yet," the waitress points out.

"I know I can't eat it all," Rachel tells her.

"Sure, Sweetheart." When you've been waiting tables for twenty years, you learn not to question what people want.

Bruce is curious about Rachel's choice.

"How come a veggie?"

Rachel searches for the right words, "I've been feeling guilty about eating meat…seems cruel."

Bruce contemplates Rachel's remarks, while Jack rolls his eyes and points at his canines. "See these? They're sharp because we're carnivores."

Rachel is not backing down. "Actually, that's not true. Do you know which land animal has the largest canines?"

Jack shrugs, "Lions?"

Not a bad guess, Bruce thinks to himself.

"It's the Hippopotamus—a herbivore," Rachel says.

Jack lets out a laugh and turns to Bruce, "I hate it when she wins with facts."

"Even if we were carnivores," Rachel continues, "we could change. We have a choice."

She remembers a quote from Paul McCartney that affected her profoundly: *"If slaughterhouses had glass walls, everyone would be a vegetarian."*

Jack can see how emotional Rachel has become. Not wanting to upset her, he extends an olive branch. "Well, at least I didn't order a veal sandwich."

"Say what?" The relevance of this remark is lost on Bruce.

Jack doesn't want to explain it and nudges Rachel, "You tell him."

"Are you sure you want to know?"

Bruce nods yes—without a clue about what Rachel means.

"Okay then. Most people don't want to hear it," she says as if a warning were required.

From her, Bruce learns that to produce veal, calves are taken from their mothers at birth and kept in pens so tight they cannot move.

Without movement, no muscle can develop and the meat is guaranteed to be tender. Some calves are slaughtered within weeks, while others are given a bit longer to live. None make it past a year.

"We separate babies from their mothers, then cage and kill them for their meat. Is there anything more horrible than that?"

Bruce is shocked to hear of such cruelty. He had no idea. In the past, he has eaten veal routinely. The thought of it now makes him ill. He cannot shake off the image of a helpless calf and, unexpectedly, it takes him to a distant memory.

He is five years old and on holiday with his parents. The sun is shining brightly on this warm summer day—perfect for a drive through the countryside. His mother spots some cows grazing in a pasture by the road, and they pull over so Bruce can have a look at the new born calf.

He had forgotten about that experience until this very moment. How could he have disconnected with what must happen to these animals for them to end up on the menu? Regretting his earlier choice, Bruce admits to Rachel, "Wish I'd ordered a veggie too."

She smiles at his support and, for an instant, it feels as if she has known him all her life.

Jack bites into his burger vigorously.

"Not me. I'm lovin' this."

Rachel divides her meal and packs half in the take-out container. She looks out the window at the homeless man and hopes that the food she has for him won't be too cold by the time they are done.

When the bill comes, Bruce is quick to reach for it. Rachel thinks they should all chip in, but Bruce insists on paying—like he always does. Jack and Rachel wonder how Bruce can be so generous and conclude that his family must be wealthy.

As they leave the restaurant, Rachel tells the boys to go ahead. She'll meet up with them later. Walking across the street, she finds the homeless man sifting through a garbage bin. He hasn't eaten all day and accepts the brown bag eagerly.

"Bless you," he says softly, revealing a mouth filled with teeth that are stained, crooked...and mostly missing. The rest of him fares no better, but Rachel only sees the gratitude in his eyes.

Jack is enthralled by their winning streak and rambles on about the solid performance of the team. He doesn't notice that Bruce is distracted.

Concerned for Rachel's safety, Bruce glances back to see her still with the homeless man, who is sitting on a bench and enjoying his dinner. The way she is standing over this man, a certain gentleness, evokes another image from his childhood.

Young Bruce and his mother are preparing to leave the house. Through the glass pane in the front door, they see that snow is falling like a sea of cotton balls. His mother has knitted a wool hat for him and pulls it down to cover his ears. "There, now you'll be all warm," she says with a hug.

"Sorry about that, guys." Rachel ran three blocks to catch up and is unaware that she just disrupted Bruce's thoughts.

Jack doesn't skip a beat. "We've never made it this far. Coach is so pumped!"

Bruce is excited about their prospects as well and lets his past slip away.

"The semis would be a great Christmas present," Jack says optimistically.

"Works for me," Bruce agrees.

"Told you already. Going all the way!" Rachel reminds them both.

Fifteen

Without a seat to spare in the school gymnasium, it feels as if every student at Lincoln were attending the semifinals.

Placton Academy, an exclusive private school, is the visiting team. Their players have personal trainers, a dedicated nutritionist, and a coach who played for the NBA. In customized outfits, their cheerleaders perform routines that have been professionally choreographed. They expect to win.

Many at Lincoln suspect that Placton is the stronger team. Nevertheless, it is loyalty first, and they will be cheering loudly for their own.

The importance of this game has been weighing on Jack's mind. Some people are at their best under pressure, while others cave under the slightest strain. Jack asks himself, *Which are you?*

Bruce senses the tension in his friend and lightens it up, "We got this."

Both of them see the coach fidgeting, but neither one mentions it.

"Our day to shine, boys," the coach says, "just like we practiced. Jack, keep your eye on Number 17."

At the mention of 17, Bruce recoils as if someone slapped him across the face. No one notices...there's too much going on.

The game kicks off with Jack and Number 17 facing each other at center. Within a matter of minutes, Number 17 pushes through to score. Disappointed in himself, Jack looks over at Bruce and shakes his head. Bruce waves his hand to send back a message: it's okay.

At halftime, Lincoln is behind by a staggering twenty points. The coach needs another play. "Bruce, you cover 17. Jack, take Bruce's spot."

It is absolutely the right call. Number 17, as good as he, is no match for Bruce. In a rhythm that has been well rehearsed, Bruce sends the ball to Jack, who knows where to wait for it.

With less than two minutes to go, the game is now tied.

This remarkable comeback is not only unexpected but abhorrent to Number 17. He is a volcano ready to erupt. When Bruce is about to make another pass, Number 17 can't help himself. He trips Bruce in mid-motion.

While falling, Bruce is forced to make a split-second decision: send the ball to Jack or take the long shot?

Bruce shoots.

Mouths drop and heads turn as all eyes fixate on the trajectory of the ball across the court. No one expects it to go in from such a distance. Still, there is hope it will. When the ball swooshes through the basket, barely grazing the rim, the crowd explodes into a hysterical frenzy. Lincoln is going to the State Finals!

Distracted by the unbelievable shot, the coach does not immediately notice that Bruce is rolling on the floor—holding his leg in pain.

Jack pounces on Number 17 and delivers a solid blow before their coaches pry them apart.

Blood drips from Number 17's nose, turning

him into a raging bull. "You're a dead man, Campbell!" he shouts with venom.

The coach from Placton, desperate not to lose his six-digit performance bonus, argues vehemently for the game to be disqualified.

Coach Wyatt may not be as highly paid as his counterpart, but he is no pushover. "Game's over, not disqualified." Pointing to the scoreboard, he states what is plain to see, "We won."

In a fit of anger, the team from Placton storms off—disregarding the tradition that players shake hands at the end of a game.

"No class," Coach Wyatt mutters under his breath.

Jack checks on Bruce.

"How you doin', bud?"

Bruce has a silly smirk on his face.

"I think the other guy's worse."

He is deeply moved by Jack's loyalty and knows it is something he will never forget.

"Got your back," Jack pledges.

You can count on me too…when the time comes, Bruce thinks to himself.

The coach examines Bruce's ankle, which has swollen to double its normal size. They need to get to a hospital as soon as possible. Since it will be faster to drive than to wait for an ambulance, the coach holds Bruce up on one side and instructs Jack to provide support on the other. The two of them manage to get Bruce to the car with Rachel holding doors open along the way.

In any hospital, the responsiveness of the Emergency department is unpredictable. It all depends on what else is happening at the same time. Thankfully, there are no car accidents, heart attacks, or other trauma cases when the four of them arrive. Two hours later, the doctor is able to provide a prognosis for Bruce.

"There is a fracture, but it's not serious. He just needs to stay off his feet for a couple of weeks."

"That's great news!" the coach says with a sigh of relief.

The doctor, however, is not finished yet. "Only problem is, seems Mr. Meyer has no next of kin."

Jack and Rachel stare at each other, taken aback by this revelation.

"Did you know that?" the coach asks Jack.

"Umm…"

Rachel sees that Jack is struggling and comes to the rescue, "Yeah, his parents were killed in a car accident."

Jack looks at Rachel incredulously, but her answer did the trick.

"Gonna be a problem. We've got two kids and the newborn. Jack, can you take Bruce for two weeks?"

"I wish I could," Jack replies with a heavy heart. "We're in LA for the holidays. Family reunion."

"He can stay with me—at my house," Rachel offers.

"That works," Jack agrees. It's the best solution for Bruce.

With the situation under control, the coach checks his watch and sees that he can still make it to his son's birthday party.

"I have get going. Tell Bruce I'm glad he's okay."

Half an hour later, with the help of aluminum crutches, Bruce emerges from the swinging doors on his own. He smiles at his two best friends—touched that they have waited for him.

Jack is eager to deliver the news, "You're

all set! Rachel has volunteered to be Florence Nightingale until you get better."

Florence Nightingale? Bruce makes a mental note to look that up later. He has no idea that this woman was a pioneer in nursing. "I'm fine. It's no big deal," he tells Jack.

"How are you getting home?" Rachel asks.

Bruce looks away to avoid eye contact. "My parents are coming to pick me up."

Rachel doesn't understand why Bruce is lying to them. "That's not happening is it? What's really going on?"

Bruce struggles; truth is not an option.

Jack jumps in, "We're your friends. You can trust us."

Deceiving people he cares about is the worst. Bruce wishes there was another way. "My parents were killed in a car accident," he says unconvincingly.

Jack is tempted to mention that Rachel used the same line, but he holds back. It's already been an exhausting day.

Rachel gives in too.

"Okay, fine. You're coming home with me.

Sixteen

Rachel did not have any preconceived ideas about where Bruce might live. Even so, a studio apartment with furniture that must have come from the Salvation Army surprises her.

Bruce was reluctant to show her his place, but what else could he do? Leaning his crutches against the wall, he removes his knapsack and retrieves a large duffel bag from under his bed.

"How about this?"

Rachel looks the bag over, "Sure, that's good." She starts to pack his pants, his shirts— embarrassed when she gets to his underwear.

Bruce notices that her face has turned several shades of red and quickly thinks of something to say, "Thanks for helping me out like this."

"I never knew you lived so...simply," Rachel tells him honestly.

Moving from foster home to foster home taught Bruce to keep his possessions to a minimum—nothing he wants to share.

"There's freedom to not having much."

"Well then, you're definitely a free man!"

Bruce smiles at her clever comeback. He had hesitated to accept her assistance but finds himself glad to have it now.

Duffle bags can be rather deceiving. They hold far more than meets the eye. Everything that Bruce needs has fit into this one bag.

Rachel pulls the zipper to close and swings the strap over her shoulder. The bag, full, is almost as big as she is—making her look like an ant hauling the remnants of a breadcrumb.

"Let me carry that," Bruce suggests, even though he already has a knapsack on his back.

"I'm fine. It's not heavy."

These words barely leave her mouth when the bag snags in the doorway and causes her to stumble backward.

Bruce, a step behind, lunges forward on his crutches to block her fall.

"Who's looking after who?" Rachel says with laughter.

If you only knew! Bruce can't help thinking to himself.

Seventeen

S ometimes things work out for no particular reason. They just do. With an injury, Bruce was worried about his ability to watch over Rachel. Now, living under the same roof, his problems are solved.

Ten Char Lee, Rachel's father, is an aircraft mechanic by trade. In Taiwan, he was in charge of a six-person team that repaired commercial and military aircraft. In this country, he looks after maintenance at the airport. Her mother, Shu Haw, was a beloved kindergarten teacher. Today, she toils in a garment factory.

These people know disappointment and hardship intimately well. Yet, their struggles have not tarnished who they are. With their daughter's friend, they are true to themselves—generous and kind.

Bruce was apprehensive about being a nuisance to Rachel and her family. The welcome he receives, however, washes away these fears. In the warmth of their home, he discovers the acceptance he has always craved. Had Bruce known how it would all turn out, he would have thanked the boy who tripped him.

At dinner, Rachel approaches Bruce timidly. "I hope it's okay. We have Chinese every night."

"I love Chinese," Bruce tells her, even though he is unfamiliar with this cuisine. It was mostly potatoes and pasta at the foster homes.

In the Taiwanese culture, a guest is served first. As such, Mrs. Lee offers her stir-fried beansprouts to Bruce before anyone else. Mr. Lee is proud of his wife's cooking and declares that her wonton soup is the best in town. Rachel has made a fresh pot of tea and pours a cup for everyone.

"It's jasmine," she tells Bruce. "I hope you like it."

Bruce doesn't usually drink tea with dinner

but gives it a try. All these years, he never knew…this beverage is delightful!

Mrs. Lee heaps more beansprouts onto Bruce's plate. "You eat more. Make you better."

Derek, Rachel's younger brother, enlightens Bruce, "According to my mom, food cures everything."

Mrs. Lee raises her eyebrows.

She caught that.

Everyone uses their own chopsticks to take what they want from the table, and it occurs to Rachel that Bruce might find this behavior unappetizing. "I hope you don't mind the double dipping."

"Double dipping with you is okay with me," Bruce answers with a grin.

Rachel giggles, and the magic of it suddenly strikes him. Her laughter was what captivated him from the start. He just didn't realize it until now.

A small dog, wagging its tail in hopes of a treat, meanders over to sit at Rachel's feet.

"Who's this?" Bruce asks.

"Meet Sammy," Rachel says while giving her dog a morsel of chicken.

Chewing his snack quickly, Sammy begs

for more—exposing a lower lip that has shifted to one side. Sammy looks like he came from a bar fight that ended badly.

Dogs love you whether you are rich or poor, sick or well, attractive or homely. In many ways, they are the embodiment of unconditional love wrapped up in a furry exterior. Bruce had wished for a puppy when he was a child, probably for this reason.

He reaches over to rub Sammy's head, "Love that smile!"

Rachel remembers the day she brought home a scrawny runt. "His jaw was dislocated when he was born. No one wanted him. Good thing he was left at the shelter."

Bruce had no idea that Sammy was rescued. It makes him think of how much he has in common with this creature.

"You must have a soft spot for strays!"

Rachel laughs at Bruce's witticism.

"They're usually four-legged."

More seriously now, she reflects on her dream. "You know what I would do if I were really rich?" Frown lines have formed between her eyes, conveying the depth of her feelings. "I'd build a sanctuary for animals." With a wistful, faraway look, she continues, "All they want is to live. They don't need a bigger TV, a faster car, or anything else…not like us."

From her, Bruce learns that a mother hen will spread her wings to shield her chicks from the rain; rabbits will pull out their fur to keep their babies warm in the winter; and pigs—playful and loving—will form lasting relationships with each other.

"Animals are more intelligent than we give them credit for. They have instincts to protect their young, and they experience pain and joy no differently than we do," Rachel tells him.

Bruce hadn't thought much about what it means to consume meat before he met Rachel. Maybe, he just didn't want to know.

"Cows cry for two weeks when their calves are taken away," she says sadly.

Bruce has given up veal, but these stories cause him to do some serious soul searching. All his life he has eaten meat, and it seemed fine. Now, he finds himself troubled by it.

"Isn't it ironic that the word *humane*—compassion and kindness toward all creatures—was the original spelling for *human?*" Rachel asks him.

Bruce nods to concur, a verbal response is not required for a rhetorical question. If only he could tell her that plant-based diets are mainstream in the future.

In forty years' time, people move away from animal-based foods for a multitude of reasons. They want to reduce their carbon footprint; they want to improve their well-being; and they want be kind.

Years from now, archaeologists will discover that gladiators, the strongest and fiercest of men, were vegetarians; and athletes, the gladiators of our day, will reveal that their strength and endurance were enhanced by a plant-based diet.

The belief that vegetables make you healthy and strong—and can help save the planet—becomes widely accepted. This change in attitude causes a third of the world to alter its behavior. *One day she will know,* Bruce thinks to himself.

"I go sleep now," Mr. Lee announces. He enjoys the time with his family, but his shift begins in a few hours.

Rachel shakes off her thoughts and says goodnight to her father.

She whispers to Bruce, "He works overnight at the airport."

Bruce understands and thanks Mr. Lee before wishing him a goodnight as well.

"No problem," Mr. Lee says to Bruce. He likes this nice boy.

After her husband departs, Mrs. Lee begins her nightly ritual. Despite a long day at the factory, she is prepared to work tirelessly into the night.

On her way up the stairs, she says to Rachel, "Come up later?"

"Sure, mom," Rachel replies.

She waits until after her mother is out of earshot to tell Bruce, "My mom does piecework for extra money. I usually help her."

Rachel's parents, like so many others, came to America for a chance at a better life. Bruce knew about their background. He just didn't realize how hardworking they were until he saw it firsthand.

"That's why I'm going to business school. I want to make enough money so my mom won't have to do this anymore."

Bruce admires Rachel's resolve, "Don't

worry. Things are going to turn out for you and your family...way better than you think."

"Wow, I like how confident you're sounding on that!"

Rachel is not suspicious in the least, but her remark makes Bruce realize he was careless.

Derek grabs his gym bag and on the way out the front door yells out, "You coming to karate?"

"No, not tonight," Rachel shouts back. "I'm staying with Bruce. Have fun."

"You take karate?" Bruce is impressed.

"Yeah. My mom wanted piano lessons for me and my brother. My dad, however, insisted that his children be able to defend themselves." Rachel launches into a mock karate move, "Guess who won?"

The war on the horizon comes to mind and Bruce becomes somber, "Your dad is a visionary."

"What do you mean?" Rachel asks, confounded by the sudden change in his demeanor.

Bruce looks down and stammers, "Nothing. Nothing really."

He messed up again!

"Actually, you're right about my dad being a visionary…in another way." Rachel explains, "When we were little, he made me and my brother read a book a week. We had to copy entire chapters each day before we could watch any television. I resented it at the time but pretty grateful for it now. When people comment on how quickly I read and write, it's really because of him."

Bruce can't help thinking, *Those private schools have nothing on Mr. Lee.*

Rachel starts to clear the table and Bruce gets up to help. He takes his plate over to the sink—finding it difficult to balance his crutches at the same time. Despite these challenges he asks, "What else can I do?"

"How about you wash the dishes by leaning on your crutches?"

Rachel hands him a cloth.

"Take this to dry."

Bruce's jaw drops.

"I'm just kidding," she teases. "You didn't think I was serious did you? Just sit and keep me company."

Bruce can't believe he fell for that! He shakes his head, laughs, and maneuvers back to his chair. On the way, he notices a black-and-white photograph on the cupboard by the wall. Intrigued, he picks it up for a closer look.

"That was taken at the airport in Taipei, the day we left to come here," Rachel tells him. "Can you believe my dad only had two hundred dollars and a dictionary in his pocket?"

"Amazing!"

Bruce suspects there's more to Mr. Lee than meets the eye.

"Yeah, I'm really proud of him. To go to a new country with no money and two kids? I can't imagine doing that!"

Staring at the skinny girl in the picture, Bruce asks, "How old are you here?"

Rachel reminisces about those early days, "I'm seven."

A look of alarm suddenly washes over Bruce's face. Just as quickly, however, it is gone...leaving Rachel to wonder why. In any case, she continues to tell him more.

"When we first came to the States, I didn't see my dad much. He had to catch three buses to get to work and was gone before I woke up."

Bruce thinks, "That's hard, but I'm sure

glad he brought you here," and then realizes that he said it out loud!

Rachel blushes, prompting Bruce to hastily add, "Or I'd be in my apartment with stale bagels!"

There is an awkwardness to this moment, but both carry on, pretending not to notice. Bruce sets down the photograph and makes his way back to the kitchen table.

"Would you mind if I put on a record?" Rachel asks. "I like music when I work."

"Absolutely! Love music."

Bruce surmises that a record must be the vinyl disc in her hand, and he's hoping that she doesn't ask him for a favorite artist or song. He could not provide a reasonable answer for 1985.

Luckily, Rachel already has something in mind. "Is the *Bee Gees Greatest* okay with you? My favorite song is on that album."

"Sure. Sounds good," Bruce says.

Out of curiosity, he asks, "What song is that?"

"'How Deep Is Your Love.' Do you like it?"

Bruce doesn't know this oldie, but that might be strange so he plays it safe, "Great song."

With the music in the background, Rachel resumes her position at the sink. She makes conversation while scraping leftovers from the plates.

"Tell me about your family."

It is not an unusual request, but Bruce tenses up. Most of his memories are painful... and he has no idea where to begin.

Sensing his hesitation, Rachel turns around and gently asks, "What really happened to your parents?"

All his life, Bruce has played his cards close to his chest, never revealing anything about himself. But Rachel, standing there with soapsuds on her hands and concern in her eyes, disarms him. If there is anyone he can trust, it is her.

He wades in slowly, "They were in the military. Both killed in action."

"Oh, Bruce, I'm so sorry."

Rachel bites her lip, remorseful now to have pushed for an explanation.

"It happened on July 7th, and I was seven years old. For most people, seven is a lucky number. Not me."

Rachel's heart breaks for him. She can't

imagine how difficult it would have been for Bruce to lose his parents at such a young age. Then, another thought enters her mind, "Number 17!"

Bruce sighs, "Exactly."

In a knee-jerk reaction, Rachel bursts out laughing. Mortified by her thoughtless behavior, she can't apologize fast enough, "I'm sorry. I'm so sorry."

Bruce has a glare in his eyes. His lips have narrowed. He looks angry.

This charade, however, is impossible to keep up; and he breaks out laughing as well. Rachel would never be hurtful...he knew that.

The response from Bruce is a relief, but it is also an eye-opener. Rachel never realized how little she really knows about him. "Do you remember them? Your parents?"

To answer her question, Bruce will have to revisit the past—a journey which has always left him empty and sad. But tonight, for some reason tonight, he doesn't feel that way; and he opens up to her with his most vivid memory.

"I made my mother a bracelet for Mother's Day. She kissed me for what felt like a hundred times and always wore it, except when she was on duty."

Rachel smiles softly at Bruce.

He smiles back.

She finishes up the dishes, wipes the counter, and walks over to sit with him.

"Sorry I was so useless," Bruce says ruefully.

"It's only a few dishes. No big deal."

Rachel usually cleans up after dinner and doesn't give it another thought. She is intrigued by Bruce's childhood.

"How about your dad?"

"My dad?"

Rachel nods.

"What do you remember about him?"

Bruce reflects on his father fondly.

"He taught me to ride my first bike. We practiced at a dead end near our house. When he let go, and I pedaled on my own, he waved so proudly—like it was the most incredible thing he had ever seen."

Rachel finds herself staring at Bruce and picturing the sweet boy he must have been.

"It's funny how our memories work. I can recall every detail of that day," Bruce says wistfully.

These stories are heartwarming and heartbreaking at the same time. Rachel would be inconsolable with the loss of her parents. For a young child, it must have been devastating. If she could reach through the years and hug that seven-year-old boy, she would.

Did he read her mind?

"This Christmas will be the first, in a long time, that I feel like I belong," Bruce says quietly.

Moved by his honesty, Rachel reveals a secret as well, "I never liked that holiday."

Bruce looks at her curiously. Doesn't everyone love Christmas?

"When we were little, my dad made me and my brother wrap Kleenex boxes to put under the tree. I was so ashamed. Someone even said, 'Aren't you lucky to have so many gifts?'"

Rachel shakes her head.

"I'll never make my kids do that. There's no shame in being poor or *alone*."

Even if she hadn't emphasized the word *alone*, Bruce would have known it was meant for him.

"Why didn't anyone ever notice that all those presents were exactly the same size? You don't have to be a genius to see that!" Rachel makes a face and giggles as if she's just heard the funniest joke.

And there it is!

How did it escape him before?

Children waiting eagerly at the ice cream truck, pajamas still warm from the dryer, flowers peeking through in the early days of spring—her laughter is all of this and more. Clear as day, Rachel took something painful and transformed it into something silly, something inconsequential. This is what Bruce finds compelling; this is what he admires most.

Negative energy flows through her, ineffective against her being, incapable of contaminating her spirit. He has never known such resilience. Loneliness, rejection, and insecurity run deep in him, veiled by a facade of self-sufficiency. What is effortless to Rachel has eluded Bruce his entire life.

She's the one who makes me safe, not the other way around, he thinks to himself.

"Speaking of presents," Rachel says with an air of mystery, "I have something for you."

Walking over to the cupboard, she returns holding a small box wrapped in silver paper and decorated with a bright green ribbon.

Glowing with excitement, she hands him her surprise.

Being able to stay with Rachel and her family was already a gift. Bruce did not expect anything else. It's embarrassing. Why didn't he pick something up for her?

Caught empty-handed, he responds with a quick-witted comment. "My box of Kleenex?"

Rachel is in a playful mood. "Let's see how you blow your nose with it."

Bruce unties the ribbon and peels back the paper. When he sees the iconic swoosh on the box, his eyes light up. *Nikes!*

"It's the Air Jordan. You'll jump higher than the sky! Okay, maybe not quite that high," she concedes.

Bruce is fully aware of the technology behind Nike shoes. It is what makes this company dominant in basketball well into the future. At West Point, all the players wore them.

Nikes, however, are not cheap…not even in 1985. Rachel works eight-hour shifts at Avis each Saturday and Sunday to make money for college yet spends a fortune on these shoes. No one else would do that for him.

"I got the same pair for Jack. You guys can

be perfectly coordinated when you bring home the State Cup!" she says confidently.

Bruce pretends to bite his fingernails.

"No pressure or anything."

"Hey, Nike got its name from the goddess of victory!" Rachel waves her hand magically, "It's a done deal. All you have to do now, is show up!"

Her optimism is infectious, making Bruce wish he could tell her that he won't let Jack down. If only he had something for her as well. Then, out of the blue, an idea comes to him.

"Wait here a minute," Bruce says as he hops over to the couch where he's been sleeping. His knapsack is on the floor, and he rummages through it before making his way back.

Rachel doesn't understand—not until Bruce shows her. In the palm of his hand is a colorful, beaded *bracelet*.

At first, she is confused.

Then, it dawns on her!

"Is this? Oh no, Bruce. I can't."

"Please, I want you to have it," he says earnestly. "It feels like I'm home...and I haven't felt that way in a long time."

Rachel hesitates.

Can she accept something so precious?

But Bruce, with a voice that could not be more sincere, insists, "Please. I really want you to have it."

In her mind, Rachel pictures the little boy offering his most prized possession; and she thinks, *How can I refuse?*

She accepts the bracelet bashfully and slips it carefully over her wrist.

"Thank you. It's...beautiful."

Bruce was able to survive the foster homes and the bullies because he is someone who looks ahead, someone who anticipates. Spontaneous behavior is a liability and, as such, something he has avoided. Yet, despite living his entire life this way, he gave Rachel the bracelet without thinking. In the moment, it felt right for her to have it. He wanted her to have it!

Now, with the bracelet on her wrist, he sees it for what it actually is: a cluster of plastic beads held together by an elastic string.

"I know it's not much...made it when I was six," Bruce says shyly.

Rachel knows that this bracelet was worn by his mother. He could not have given her anything more valuable.

"I will treasure it…always."

On impulse, she lifts up on her tiptoes and kisses him. All the feelings she could not explain or understand find their outlet through this kiss. An electric current runs through her entire body when her lips touch his. It is as if she has never truly kissed before.

Was it the same for him?

She pulls away and looks into his eyes.

Reflecting back at her is a boy who appears awkward and uneasy. All at once, Bruce seems unfamiliar.

Her heart refuses to believe her eyes. She searches his face again. Still…nothing. There is not a single hint that he likes her this way. Not one.

"I'm sorry. I'm so sorry." Rachel feels sick to her stomach. If a hole could be found in her kitchen, she would crawl into it. After blurting out a quick thank-you, she flees to her bedroom, stumbling over the stairs in her haste.

There was no choice. Bruce had to pretend that he felt nothing, and he loathes himself for it.

Did he give Rachel the bracelet to draw her

closer? Was it what he wanted all along without admitting it to himself?

If only he could tell her—tell her that he can't stop thinking about her—that he wants to hold her in his arms and never let go. What has he done! He should run after her…but he can't.

Eighteen

Although Bruce only stayed with Rachel for two weeks, their relationship can never be the same again. What was purely platonic has become much more. None of it was intentional…but it happened anyway.

At lunch in the school cafeteria, Jack tells Rachel and Bruce that he missed them both despite enjoying the time with his cousins. He has no idea they did not think of him once.

"So, how was the Lee Hotel?" Jack asks.

"Top notch. Five stars all the way," Bruce replies, careful not to say more.

"Thought so." Jack knows Rachel's parents would be gracious to anyone.

"Poor guy," Rachel says. "We had Chinese every night."

"Are you kidding me?" Bruce smacks his lips, "I'm craving that wonton soup already." With humor, he is trying to get back to where they were before *the kiss*. It is an attempt to put the pieces back together.

There was, however, a nursery rhyme he heard as a child: *"Humpty Dumpty sat on a wall, Humpty Dumpty had a great fall. All the kings' horses and all the kings' men couldn't put Humpty together again."*

"Come over anytime," Rachel offers. "My parents love you!"

Bruce breaks into a sweat…it's the last thing he wanted her to say.

"Hey!" Jack objects, "What about me?"

Rachel isn't falling for the drama. She knows her boyfriend is joking.

"They like you too, but we know how you feel about Chinese food."

Jack shrugs; it's true. Fried rice is about the only thing he will eat.

This discussion and where it could lead makes Bruce uneasy. Subtly, he redirects the conversation, "Have you guys decided where you're going next year?"

"I applied to Stanford. My grandfather went there," Jack says proudly.

Bruce had no idea that his friend came from such distinguished lineage. He thinks about his own grandparents—strangers who rejected him.

"My parents would be happy for sure." Jack goes on to say, "Stanford is a long-standing tradition for us."

Rachel has remained silent even though she knows how much this university means to the Campbell family.

"Thing is, even if I did get in, it's a lot of money. My dad was helping his brother with a restaurant, but it went bankrupt. We lost our savings. I'm going to need that basketball scholarship."

Jack doesn't want sympathy and quickly adds, "Whatever, it's no big deal. There's lots of other options." He sounds ambivalent—fooling no one.

"You're going to get that scholarship!" Rachel insists. Scouts will be at the championships and she could have, but does not, point out that the team's chances of making it there are excellent with Bruce. Some things are better left unsaid.

Jack has shared more than he wanted and deflects the attention to Rachel.

"Can you believe she's abandoning me? Something about Columbia having a decent business school."

Rachel did not set out to leave her boyfriend. She chose Columbia University for a reason. Warren Buffet and Prem Watsa—two investors for whom she has great respect—follow the teachings of Benjamin Graham, a past professor there.

In the 1920s, when investing was rife with speculation, Ben Graham believed that research could determine the intrinsic value of a company and its share price. His textbook *Security Analysis*, coauthored with David Dodd, is a timeless classic. As such, Columbia is known for value investing, and it is the program that she has in mind.

The decision to attend a college across the country was difficult for Rachel. It's not just Jack, she will be leaving her family and Bruce as well. In the end, despite being torn, she chose to follow her dreams.

"How about we stay in touch with this

device called *the telephone*? It's been around for years."

Rachel thought she was being funny. The grimace on Jack's face, however, indicates quite the opposite. She didn't mean to hurt his feelings and moves swiftly to repair the injury.

"You're going to be so busy, it'll be like Rachel? Who? Besides, I'm back for the holidays—Christmas and Spring break too. We'll be okay."

Jack is disappointed that his girlfriend won't be within driving distance, but it does not, in any way, diminish how proud he is of her.

"Rachel has the academic scholarship nailed down," he tells Bruce. "How is 98 percent even possible? She's been a brain since grade four, even though she couldn't speak a word of English two years before that."

Rachel smiles awkwardly.

There are people who are inherently gifted, naturally clever...not her. She works hard for those marks, the ticket to higher education and a better life for her and her family. A part-time job covers tuition. It's not enough for residence, books, food, and other expenses. She needs that scholarship.

Rachel's academic standing is news to Bruce. In all their times together, it never came up.

"Grade four?"

He isn't sure he heard Jack correctly.

"Yep. She was in my class."

"Wow, didn't know you guys went back that far," Bruce says, feeling a twinge of jealousy

"It's funny, but I don't remember when she became my girlfriend. We kind of always knew each other."

Rachel nods to agree with Jack. She can't recall the day they became a couple either.

"Remember Miss Moore?"

"Bruce doesn't want to hear that," Rachel says dismissively.

Jack, however, is just getting started and launches into his story with great gusto.

"We had this teacher, Miss Moore, and for some reason she didn't like Rachel. That's weird, right? Teachers usually like smart kids. Less for them to do."

"Jack!" Rachel cries out, but he is on a roll.

"Miss Moore had a contest to see how many words we could make from the letters of *Supercalifragilisticexpialidocious*. And guess what? Rachel came up with 250, I had 45, and everyone else less than that. Miss Moore didn't believe Rachel and scrutinized her work—which was perfect of course. No congratulations or anything. Rachel blew the class away like she always does."

Shaking her head, Rachel appears to be denying that it ever happened. The truth is, she stayed up all night with a dictionary to extract every last word.

Jack warns Bruce, "Don't be fooled by this innocent-looking girl."

Rachel objects again—to no avail.

"The only thing I can do better than her," Jack says while mimicking a free throw, "is this."

He turns to Bruce, "You too."

"I believe that," Bruce agrees humbly.

Rachel loves the chemistry between the three of them. *I wish it could be like this forever,* she thinks to herself. *All for one and one for all.*

If there were a contest for bad timing, Kora would win first prize. She spots Bruce in the cafeteria and heads straight to him with a tray full of mini-pizzas and chocolate milk.

"Hi, Rachel. Hi, guys." Kora's greeting presumes that they are old friends...which they are not. There isn't an empty seat on the bench, but she squeezes in anyway—forcing Rachel to slide over.

Pizza is Kora's favorite and she gorges on her pepperoni and cheese special. In her haste, she nearly gags and quickly gulps down a mouthful of chocolate milk. Not all the food has washed away when she says, "Great game, Bruce. You were awesome!"

Dripping with adoration that is thicker than day-old cream, her infatuation could not be more obvious. Jack nudges Bruce, who is not enjoying the innuendo.

Kora pushes forward to execute the blueprint of her plan, "How about a movie this weekend?"

"You've got a fan," Jack whispers to Bruce—as if he didn't know!

The attention from Kora is awkward and unwarranted. Bruce has seen her with Rachel at the games. Nothing more.

"Saturday's good, right? No game?" Rachel suggests.

The last thing that Bruce wants is to spend time with Kora, but how to stop this freight train?

"Let's see the one with Michael J. Fox," Kora says excitedly. "I just love him!"

Jack thinks he knows the movie she is talking about, *Back to the Future?*

"Yeah, that's it. It's so cool. He goes back in time and ends up fixing his future."

Bruce does a double take. *What? No way!*

"The reviews have been really good." Rachel knows how persistent Kora can be and hopes her comment will help the boys agree.

"Let's go then," Jack says.

Kora smiles at Bruce. "Can you pick me up?"

Jack winks at Bruce before suddenly yelling out, "Ouch!" Bruce just kicked him under the table.

Nineteen

Back to the Future is the highest-grossing film in 1985 for a reason. This movie is imaginative, fun, and clever. Bruce, however, would have enjoyed watching anything on the big screen. In the darkness, where action, romance, comedy, and drama unfold, he can be distracted from his worries...for a while.

At the AMC Theatre, Kora leads the way to seats in the back row. She wants to sit beside Bruce and directs Jack to go in first, followed by Rachel. When the lights dim, Jack puts his arm over his girlfriend. Kora is waiting for Bruce to do the same with her, but he appears oblivious to it all.

After the previews have been shown, Kora grows impatient. It will be up to her to make the first move. Wriggling as close to Bruce as the armrest in between them will allow, she nestles her head on his shoulder.

Bruce can feel the goosebumps rise on his skin. Attraction cannot be forced or rushed. Unfortunately, no one told Kora.

"Popcorn anyone?" Bruce is desperate for an escape.

"Sure, I'll take some. Thanks!" If Bruce is offering, Jack is jumping on it.

Rachel thinks about how expensive popcorn is at the theatre and tells Bruce that she can share with Jack.

With a stiff pout, Kora grumbles, "Why didn't you get it before the show started?"

"You don't want to know," Bruce mutters under his breath.

When he returns, juggling bags of popcorn and cups of soda, he has missed the beginning of the film. Even so, it is not difficult to piece together the storyline: any deviation from the past, however trivial, can result in a future that is dramatically altered. These unforeseen consequences amuse and delight the audience. For Bruce, it is a reminder of the risks to saving his parents.

At the end of the movie, the crowd whistles and applauds. It rarely happens. Kora gloats from ear to ear. After all, the show was her choice—and she is quick to point that out.

Bruce wonders, *Am I the only one who finds her annoying?*

Without school the next day, the four of them opt for dessert at a nearby coffee shop. Taking a shortcut through a lane behind the theatre, they find themselves confronted by five boys blocking the way.

"No one to save your butt now, Campbell!"

It's Number 17, without the nosebleed, but with the same fire in his eyes. He has brought his gang to seek revenge for a game they should have won.

Bruce sizes up the situation. He can take these amateurs; Rachel is his worry. Instinctively, he tells her and Kora to run.

Jack agrees, "Go, Rachel!"

A frightened Kora makes a dash for it. She doesn't glance back to see if Rachel is following behind. Kora is not waiting for anyone.

Rachel refuses to abandon the boys. Planting her feet solidly into the ground, she declares, "I'm staying."

Bruce is frantic. Why won't she go!

Suddenly, he is seized by a thought, *Is this the reason I was sent back?*

Number 17 charges at Jack. It is a dirty, ugly fight between these two. Neither one possess any combat skills and go at each other with brute force.

Two boys, taking the cue from Number 17, close in on Bruce. Bruce steps in front of Rachel, grabs the first boy by the arm, and flips him over his shoulder. Following through with a sharp blow to the chest, Bruce makes sure this boy stays down. Not to waste a minute, Bruce immediately turns his attention to the second boy. He can't believe his eyes! That boy is struggling to hold his own against Rachel.

The remaining two boys see that Bruce is distracted and use this opportunity to ambush him. They have no idea what they are up against. One is elbowed in the head, while the other is kicked in the groin. Both end up squirming on the ground—in fetal positions.

Now, as Bruce checks on Rachel, he is astounded by what he sees. She is in mid-air with a spinning back kick that strikes her opponent in the temple. That boy never saw what hit him.

In the meantime, Jack and Number 17 continue to slug it out. Frustrated that it has not been an easier fight, Number 17 retrieves a switchblade from his back pocket.

Jack is defenseless against a knife.

Not Bruce. He kicks the weapon away from Number 17's hand and strikes him in the throat with an open palm. Number 17 drops to his knees, gasping for air.

"I could have killed you," Bruce warns him.

Two of the boys, now back on their feet, offer assistance to their ringleader. He pushes them away. His pride has been wounded enough.

Bruce glares at them with an unspoken message: *Don't mess with us again!*

The five boys limp away, unsure of how they were so completely defeated.

"You guys okay?" Bruce asks his friends.

Blood drips from Jack's nose and he wipes it off with his sleeve. "Where'd you learn to fight like that?"

"I have a black belt in Judo and trained for hand-to-hand combat," would be the truthful answer. Instead, Bruce tells Jack, "I grew up in foster homes. Had to defend myself."

Rachel's performance is what Bruce really wants to talk about. "Were you in *Crouching Tiger, Hidden Dragon?*" he teases.

"Huh?" Rachel stares at Bruce, open-mouthed.

Of course! That movie, garnering an Academy Award for Best International Feature Film in the year 2000, has not been made yet!

Bruce glances down, scrambling for an excuse to conceal his blunder. "Um, I was just referring to a show about women in karate." It's lame, but he had nothing else.

Rachel sees that Bruce is avoiding eye contact and suspects there is more behind his comment. Regardless, she lets it go. Too much has happened already.

"Good thing you were with us," Jack says to Bruce.

"Got your back," Bruce tells his friend. By habit, he offers his fist for their knuckle punch.

"Ouch!" Jack cries out. It was not the smartest move with a bruised hand.

Now that the tension is gone, both boys laugh at this oversight.

The bond between Bruce and Jack was strong before. This incident, however, brings them even closer—in a way that soldiers who have gone to war together understand.

Twenty

As with most nights, Mrs. Lee is bent over an industrial-sized sewing machine in the small den on the second floor of her house. Typically, she will complete ten dresses before going to bed—a feat unsurpassed by anyone else at the factory where she works ten-hour days.

Mrs. Lee does not know about Henry Ford and how he revolutionized auto production by the use of an assembly line. On her own, she has figured out that a dress can be completed in half the time if all the pieces are sewn continuously and put together at the end.

Rachel's job is to separate the pieces and regroup them so her mother can work without interruption. It is something that Rachel has done ever since she can remember.

In the privacy of this moment, she confides in her mother—speaking in Taiwanese, "I'm so confused."

Mrs. Lee stops sewing and looks up at her daughter, whose troubled voice requires attention.

"It doesn't make sense, but I don't know if I like Jack or Bruce better."

Mrs. Lee met her husband through an arranged marriage. What advice could she give about boys?

"That's hard. They're both nice," is all she can think of to say.

"I know," Rachel agrees. "I've been with Jack forever, yet I feel closer to Bruce. How can that be?"

Mrs. Lee is expected to deliver another five dresses the next day. It forces her to speak and sew at the same time. "I wish I could tell you. Only you know. I like them both."

"Jack's a good person. It's just that I'm really happy when I'm with Bruce."

Rachel has been struggling with this dilemma for some time. She may be asking her mother for advice but, the truth is, she just wanted someone to talk to.

Mrs. Lee has rarely seen her daughter so upset. She thinks about her own life and how unpredictable it was. Perhaps if she tells Rachel that things happen for a reason, it will be helpful.

"When I was a young girl, someone showed me a postcard of San Francisco with the Golden Gate Bridge. At the time, I never thought I would see this beautiful place for myself. Now, it's where we live. You'll know what to do... when you're ready."

"That's okay," Rachel says softly. "Bruce doesn't feel the same about me anyway.

Twenty-One

The coach steps up the duration and frequency of practice games which would normally be met with moans and groans. A shot at the state championship, however, doesn't come around everyday. Hence, there are no complaints about getting up before the sun rises.

"To beat anyone, in any sport, you need to be more prepared than your opponent." This mantra from the coach translates into training that includes a regimen of laps, weights, and push-ups even before the practice game begins. These boys are in excellent shape, and they know it.

"Being physically strong makes you mentally strong," the coach reiterates. He is convinced that victories are gained by a state of mind as much as they are by technical ability.

After two hours of grueling drills and playing hard, the boys need a shower before heading to class. On the way to the change room, Jack notices the burgundy swoosh on Bruce's running shoes and remarks, "Was there a two-for-one sale?"

"Maybe," Bruce tells him, "but I have a good feeling about them."

"Yeah, me too," Jack agrees. "Leave it to Rachel to think of everything."

Bruce nods to concur and hopes his friend doesn't read more into it than that.

"I gave her a Timex," Jack says, "to remember our times together."

Bruce is impressed, "Great line."

"I needed a good line because it's a pretty cheap watch!"

"I'm sure she loves it."

"Did you get her anything?"

"Umm...no, I didn't."

Bruce regrets the lie as soon as it is spoken, but what could he have said? I gave her a bracelet made by a six- year old?

Jack sees that he has put Bruce on the spot.

It was not his intention. "Don't worry. She wasn't expecting anything from you."

Both boys are almost at the change room when the coach calls out, "Mr. Campbell."

"Right there, Coach!" Jack will have to catch up with Bruce later.

The coach lowers his voice as Jack approaches, "I wanted to speak to you privately."

"Sure thing, Coach." Close up, Jack sees Mr. Wyatt is clutching his hands.

"You know Scouts are coming to the finals, right?"

"Yeah, I know," Jack replies casually, even though he has thought of nothing else.

"I hear you could use a scholarship," the coach says directly.

Jack shrugs; it's awkward.

"Lincoln has come a long way thanks to you and Bruce," the coach says proudly. He takes a full breath, lets out a sigh, and compels himself to continue with what is difficult...if not unethical.

"Every year, my goal is to bring home the state cup. We're looking good so far, but frankly, with Bruce, the scouts may not notice you as much."

Jack shakes his head.

"What are you saying, Coach?"

Sometimes it is easier to pull the Band-Aid off quickly.

"I can play Bruce less and only when you're on. Wanted to run that by you before the big game."

Jack draws a blank. There's no way his coach just said that! After a few seconds, when he has made sense of it, Jack speaks from his heart, "I can't do that to Bruce. He's my friend."

A flashback of Bruce kicking the knife away from Number 17 enters Jack's mind, and he is compelled to add, "My best friend."

What Jack does not know is that his coach was once a high school student with a future hanging on the thread of a basketball scholarship as well.

Ted Wyatt comes from a long line of miners. His father, like the fathers of so many of his friends, died from inhaling coal dust for 20 years.

Ted can still hear his mother's pleas, "Do what you have to do to get out of here!"

Without the basketball scholarship, Ted would be down in the mines today. His narrow escape from a lifetime of drudgery was made possible by a small town gym teacher who took a promising student under his wing…a debt that must be repaid.

In a million years, Jack could never have imagined that his coach would compromise the game for anyone or anything. Clearly, there is more to the man than he thought.

"I appreciate you looking out for me," Jack tells him sincerely, "but we got this."

It feels as if the roles have reversed, because it is Jack who is patting the coach on the back.

A minute ago, Mr. Wyatt was a plant that hadn't been watered in days. Now, he stands tall—the weight of the world lifted from his shoulders.

Both men walk away with their heads held high and their thoughts filled with a new understanding of each other.

Twenty-Two

There is not an empty seat to watch the game between Lincoln High and Cedarvale Collegiate for the state title. Even the principal, who is notoriously frugal, finds room in his budget for Lincoln's players and cheerleaders to be outfitted with spanking new uniforms.

Crisp-looking jerseys and matching shorts in the school colors of burgundy and white work their magic on the team's morale. Everyone at Lincoln feels like a winner today.

Cedarvale has enjoyed an impressive string of victories. Their players are intimidating. Even so, Bruce could run circles around them if he were unconstrained. Lincoln needs to win— but with Jack taking the credit. Pulling this off will be tricky.

Scouts from across the country have come to discover fresh talent. With so much at stake, the tension in the air is as thick as a London fog.

Bruce is careful to set up plays that make Jack look like the hero. Rachel can see what Bruce is doing and admires him greatly for it. On this important date, Jack comes through with his best game. He resists the temptation to look up at the scouts, though they are on his mind the entire time.

The score is nail-bitingly close—a coin toss right up until the final few minutes. As the buzzer is about to sound, Jack dodges his guard and sends the ball swooshing through the net with a classic hook shot.

Lincoln just won by two points!

In the midst of thunderous applause and a standing ovation, the cheerleaders perform their well-rehearsed routines.

Three scouts have their eye on Jack Campbell and are prepared to make an offer for him. From a distance, Bruce gives his friend the thumbs-up. Rachel hangs back too. This moment belongs to Jack.

Bruce points at his Nikes and says to Rachel, "It was the shoes."

"Absolutely," she agrees, "the only reason!"

With that comment, they both burst into laughter. If ever a day was perfect, this would be it. Bruce cannot remember the last time he was so entirely happy.

Twenty-Three

Mrs. Campbell purchased the largest turkey she could find at Walmart. Thanksgiving was long ago, but there is another reason to celebrate. Early in the morning, she started polishing the silver and arranging the place settings. Tonight needs to be perfect.

Seated at the dining table with his best friends, Bruce is overcome by the warmth of the gathering. Turning to Mr. and Mrs. Campbell, he thanks them sincerely for including him.

"We need to celebrate you kids!" Mr. Campbell announces.

Mrs. Campbell agrees wholeheartedly, "That's right, dear."

"First the championship and then a

basketball scholarship!" Mr. Campbell lifts his glass with vigor, "Congratulations everyone!"

"Don't forget Rachel's scholarship to Columbia!" Mrs. Campbell reminds her husband.

"Of course. Yes, of course. Rachel, Jack, Bruce, I'm proud of all you kids."

This meal was meticulously prepared. Five hours ago, Mrs. Campbell put the turkey in the oven and was pleased to see that it turned out perfectly—golden brown on the outside and tender on the inside. Now, with all the talking, she is worried her timing will be undermined.

Gently, she suggests, "Let's eat before the food gets cold."

As is tradition, Mr. Campbell carves the turkey and places a few slices on each plate to pass around. This dinner and how it is served could not be more different than what transpired at Rachel's house. Yet, to Bruce, it feels the same. *These people are my family,* he realizes. *The food doesn't matter.*

Mr. Campbell knows that his son was disappointed about going to Stanford without Bruce. He is curious about this young man and asks, "What are your plans?"

"Nothing to report, sir." Distracted by his thoughts, Bruce answers as if he were still at West Point.

Rachel and Jack look at each other dumbfounded. Where did that come from?

Aware of his misstep, Bruce follows up in a more laid-back manner.

"The stock market is interesting. I'm just not sure."

"That's quite all right." Mr. Campbell sympathizes with Bruce, "It's not easy to know what you're meant to do."

"You weren't sure what you wanted to do for the longest time either," his wife points out.

"She's right," he confesses. "My father wanted me to be a lawyer like him."

Jack jumps in, "Tell him about Uncle Eddie."

Mr. Campbell smiles. He knows why his son is bringing this up.

"I had a best friend in high school…like you and Jack. There were bullies at our school, and we teamed up to fight them."

Bruce and Jack have the same thought: *Number 17.*

"Somehow, word got out that the bullies were afraid of us and before we knew it, kids started coming to Eddie and me for protection. It was what made us decide to enroll in the police academy."

Mr. Campbell casts his eyes downward and mindlessly stirs the carrots on his plate. Not a day goes by that he doesn't miss his dear friend, and the quiver in his voice betrays the depths of his sorrow.

"A few years ago, Eddie was killed trying to break up a fight."

"Now, now, we're celebrating here," Mrs. Campbell interjects. "Jack's going to Stanford on a scholarship!"

Grateful for the intervention from his wife, Mr. Campbell shakes off his malaise. "That's right! Good thing someone in this family's got brains!"

Bruce Meyer

Twenty-Four

Balloons and streamers decorate the gymnasium for the much-anticipated prom. Winning the state championship is still fresh on everyone's mind, and school spirit at Lincoln could not be higher. Boys in tuxedos and girls in long gowns have come together to celebrate the end of high school and the beginning of something they expect to be much greater.

Weeks ago, I agreed to be Kora's date. It's not because I like her; I would have gone with anyone.

This is the day! I can read the message from Tom Waites today!

First thing in the morning, I checked the letter. Nothing! There was nothing!

Now I'm at the prom, plagued by a sense of helplessness. How will I protect Rachel?

All I can do is keep my eyes on her and stay alert. Fortunately, she is wearing a long white dress which stands out in the dark. It's lovely and I was surprised to learn that her mother made it from a lace tablecloth.

"I just had to buy the zipper and some ribbon," Rachel tells me, "for a whopping five dollars!"

I look down at my Nikes…that's where her money went.

Jack has rented a black tuxedo with satin trim. His rose-colored bow tie and cummerbund have been chosen to match Rachel's sash. No one can deny—they make a handsome couple.

I'm in a sports jacket with my best shirt and tie. The scorn on Kora's face, however, sends an unmistakable message about her assessment of my attire. She has splurged on a gown by Louie, Gucci, or something like that. I can't remember exactly what she said…only that I was expected to be impressed.

Fashion is not my area of expertise, but I do know that when you find someone unattractive, a designer dress makes no difference. In any case, these are trivial matters. Tonight is crucial.

The uncertainty puts me on edge and a crowded, stuffy room only makes it worse.

We're told the air-conditioning has been turned to maximum, but it sure doesn't feel that way. I don't remember the gym ever being this hot, not even for the final game.

Jack takes his jacket off and suggests we move closer to the fans, which have been brought in for additional ventilation.

I readily agree; I'm burning up.

Rachel brushes her hair away from her face and something familiar catches my eye. It's the bracelet! Hidden by the corsage on her wrist, I didn't notice it earlier.

I'm touched that she would wear a childish piece of jewelry to the prom. If Jack were not standing nearby, I would tell her so. Under the circumstances, I resort to offering her a smile. She smiles back, acknowledging the unspoken words.

Jack catches this interchange without giving it much thought. He puts his arm over Rachel and declares, "What a year!"

I couldn't be more pleased for my friend and cheer him on, "You're the man!" We knuckle punch each other, a ritual for both of us by now.

"Who knew we'd take the state title before Bruce showed up! You were right all along," he admits to Rachel.

She is quick to respond, "Fortune-teller, remember?"

Jack grins at her remark, while Kora crosses her arms and taps her feet...Morse code for *I'm bored*.

"I need a Diet Coke with lots of ice," she demands of me.

I'm reluctant to leave Rachel for a second but, desperately parched, I could use a drink myself. Wiping away the sweat running down the side of my face, I ask, "Anyone else want something?"

It's warm for everyone, but Rachel notices that I'm perspiring unusually.

"You okay?" she whispers to me.

Obsessed with her safety, I didn't pay attention to what was heating me up.

It's coming from my breast pocket!

Excusing myself immediately, I bolt into the hallway and retrieve the letter. Miraculously, the page is full:

> You were sent to protect her—not because she will save the world. You were sent because I loved her, because you love her, because we are the same person.

I'm stunned. What is he saying? It doesn't make any sense. My hands tremble so badly that it's hard to hold the paper steady. Nevertheless, I don't stop reading:

> I waited forty years for you, for me, to have another chance. Each night, I am haunted by watching her die. When the song, "How Deep Is Your Love" comes on, you must act quickly and take Rachel away from the gymnasium.

"Oh my God!" I blurt out.

And it's her song too!

> The shooter is a teacher who was dismissed after being diagnosed with paranoid schizophrenia. He will fire

into the crowd and turn the gun on
himself. You/I have been here before.
My original mission was to assassinate
Jack and make it look like an accident.
But I couldn't do it, not after I got to
know him and not after what happened
to Rachel. Then I realized I could wait.
I could wait for time to pass...to come
back again.

Immersed in the message, I don't notice a
boy coming around the corner until he bumps
into me.

"Sorry," he says, jolting me from my
thoughts.

I almost drop the letter. Frantic to get back
to reading, I wave him away with no harm
done. Looking down, I'm not aware of two girls
who have come up to me.

"Remember us?"

"We're the cheerleaders."

"You were great!"

"What are you doing next..."

My mind screams, *There's no time for this!*

"Sorry," I shout back at them while fleeing
to the men's restroom for privacy.

I hid my identity to become any Tom, Dick, or Harry…and I waited.

Tom Waites/waits. Of course!
So obvious that no one could see it.

I took advantage of major turning points in the stock and real estate markets. I invested with Jeff Bezos, Elon Musk, Mark Zuckerberg, Larry Page, and Sergey Brin. I became rich, powerful, and untouchable. With this new-found wealth, I built a reclusive haven on a private island. I needed to contrive the existence of a parallel universe to convince General Emmerson to alter his mission for Bruce Meyer—for you— for me.

My eyes are glued to the page as I grapple with the realization that I am Tom Waites!

If you're reading this, then I was successful. The general has sent you to save Rachel.

Could I have planned all of this?
It seems inconceivable.

> There is no other reality. This is it. You and I, we have the one thing that most people can only dream of: a second chance.

I'm awestruck and struggle to keep up with the pace of these revelations.

> I had to wait for you to be born, to grow up, to go to West Point—as I knew you would. With all the time in the world to think and rethink this, I still cannot tell you what to do about Rachel. I know how you feel about her. It is precisely how I felt about her forty years ago. Each night, she is the girl I see when I close my eyes. But the war begins in Jack's second term unless you take action. You know Rachel. You know she would be an asset to him. The two of them, together, could make a difference.

Rachel smiling at me with soap suds on her hands; Rachel laughing after tripping in my doorway; Rachel accepting the bracelet and slipping it shyly over her wrist—countless images fill my mind.

You choose whether or not to give her up. I'm fine with whatever you decide because either way, she lives! She lives, and that is what is most important to me...to us. Your decision will not be easy. For me / for you, there is no one else.

I fixate on the letter. Though I have never been in a boxing ring, these words are body blows.

I couldn't tell you before now—the risks were too high. You needed to act exactly the same as me, exactly the same as yourself, so that everything would be exactly as it was leading up to the prom. Once you save Rachel, the future will be reset and impossible to change again. To help her and Jack, remember that information is wealth and power. Make use of your knowledge wisely.

I become as rich and powerful as Tom Waites? Hard to believe. But if he is me, then I've already done it.

One final thing. Arrange to have a
blood transfusion as soon as possible.
You were injected with a time-release
toxin to kill you a few weeks after high
school—after you've outlived your
usefulness. I discovered it, regrettably
not in time to prevent the nerve damage
that causes me to walk with a limp.

I remember the injection that was intended
to help me acclimatize. All lies.

There is nothing left to tell you, except
to trust your instincts. They will serve
you well.

Twenty-Five

The ink disappears and staring back at me is a blank piece of paper. All at once, I am seized by the urgency of the situation. Racing back to the gym, I hear the DJ announce, "We have a special request."

Think, I tell myself, *think clearly. Don't panic.* But I am overwhelmed by fear—the kind that makes deer freeze in headlights.

Find her!

I scan the room, looking for that long white dress. The loud speakers reveal the first few notes of a song I know—"How Deep Is Your Love."

"No!" I cry out.

My head feels like it's going to explode.

Then, I see a swirl of white. Rachel is dancing with Jack at the far end of the room!

I run like lighting to her, but someone grabs my arm and yanks me back.

It's Kora—fuming like a steam engine.

"Where have you been? And where's my drink?"

I shake her loose and pull away.

"Get back here! Jerk!"

Kora's words roll off my back. Rachel is my entire focus and I blast through anyone in my way to her.

A sharp bang punctures the air.

Most people don't know the sound of a gunshot. I do.

The DJ, felled like a tree, topples over the record player and causes a grinding screech to fill the room.

The shooter now waves his weapon at the crowd. Without rhyme or reason, he pulls the trigger and sets in motion the demise of his next victim. Standing a few inches one way or the other can mean the difference between life and death.

I leap forward, shielding Rachel with my body and knocking Jack over in the process.

Three more shots are fired at random before the shooter saves the last round for himself. His final act is to point the barrel against his temple.

Mayhem takes over.

Screaming, shouting, and wailing add to the hysteria. Students and teachers scramble in confusion. Some are knocked over while others are trampled in a rush for the exit.

Bullets spear through the air without prejudice. The force of a flying dagger throws me forward, but I feel no pain—only relief. Immense, joyous, sweeping relief. Whatever else happens does not matter. She is safe.

Twenty-Six

Having recently been to the hospital for my ankle injury, Jack and Rachel are familiar with the layout and locate me easily. I'm reading a paperback with my arm and shoulder well supported by a sling when they enter my room.

"How come we keep bringing you here?" Jack says with a smirk.

I put my book down and answer, "Accident prone."

Rachel moves closer to me—wanting to see how I am for herself. "Are you okay?" she asks with concern.

"It's nothing," I assure her, "just a flesh wound."

"You can't kill Bruce with a single bullet." Jack delivers perfectly...as if he were serious.

Despite the grins on both our faces, Rachel is not amused. "No arguments. You're staying with me."

It is the first time I've seen her so stern, and I know not to argue.

Jack, true to himself, lightens the mood with a harmless jab. "Man, what some people will do to check into the Lee Hotel!"

Twenty-Seven

After dinner, Rachel and I find ourselves alone at the kitchen table once again. We are both acutely aware of what happened there last time, but neither one is comfortable enough to bring it up. Instead, the space between us is filled with inconsequential small talk.

Finally, she can't stand the frivolous chatter and speaks her mind, "Okay, tell me now."

"Tell you what?" I ask innocently.

"You know," she says.

I pretend not to understand.

"Know what?"

She looks at me with *Really?*

"You came running at us before any shots were fired. How did you know?"

"I didn't. I saw the gun and ran toward

you." With that response, I'm hoping she will let it go.

She doesn't.

"How did you know he was going to shoot us?"

"I didn't. I was only trying to protect you."

In the past, Rachel has not pressed me for the truth. It feels different this time.

"I'm just going to say it, Bruce. When you lie, you have this thing you do with your eyes. You did it when you told us your parents were killed in a car accident, and you're doing it now!"

With all my training, you'd think I could improvise on the spot. Not so. My mind has gone blank, and I am unable to think of a single thing to say—nothing that would make sense anyways. Maybe I just don't want to lie to her anymore. I don't know.

Giving in to the person from whom I have never been able to hide, I inhale deeply and let it out, "That bad?"

"Being a bad liar is a good thing," she assures me. "Only please, please tell me what is really going on."

To tell her the truth, I have to disobey a

direct order. I have to go against all that I know and trust.

Has suppressing my feelings for her depleted my resolve? Or, has knowledge of the upcoming war become a burden so heavy and so onerous that I, unknowingly, yearn to share it?

Regardless of the reason, I do not have the will to deceive her anymore. This is the moment I abandon my past—the moment I let myself fall—because Rachel is the net below.

Does the truth set us free?

"You won't believe it."

"Give me a try," she says tenderly.

Secrecy is paramount and, though I trust her, I make a point of emphasizing that she cannot tell anyone.

"Not Jack. Not your parents. No one."

"Okay, okay. I promise."

She is anxious to hear more.

"I'm from the future. I was sent to—" I can't let her know how I feel—"I was sent to protect you."

"To protect me? The future?"

Rachel is not sure she heard correctly.

"Yes," I tell her, adding reluctantly, "You

would have been killed. I couldn't let that happen."

Her eyes enlarge with astonishment. I can only imagine the thoughts running through her head. She must want to know about her family, her future, her life—I'm prepared to answer anything.

"Who are you?"

I didn't expect that.

The gates have flung open; the horses have galloped away. There is no stopping this stampede. I might as well be candid.

"I come from the year 2025. I was sent back before, but I couldn't save you then. I didn't know what was going to happen."

Rachel shakes her head in disbelief.

"You were sent back before? I don't understand."

It is complicated, so I start over.

"My original mission was to kill Jack Campbell so he never becomes president. I was sent to rewrite history, but I couldn't do it—not after I got to know him and you. Then, I realized there was another chance to make it right. In precisely forty years, the general would send a young cadet, Bruce Meyer, me, back in time to terminate the future president."

"That's crazy! It can't be!" she exclaims, overwhelmed like a computer that's run out of capacity for the amount of data being downloaded. Her eyes delve into me as if I were a total stranger, but mine is a face she knows, a face she trusts, a face that is reflecting absolute sincerity. She knows when I'm lying, and I'm not lying!

"After you died, I mapped out a plan to come back. Under an assumed identity, I arranged for a letter to be given to my younger self. That's how I knew what was going to happen and what was needed to save you."

Rachel stammers, "Jack, president?"

I nod to confirm.

"First you die. Weeks later, his father is killed while responding to a robbery. Jack is devastated. In his grief, he searches for meaning and finds it in public service. His path to the White House originates from the loss of those he loves."

"Oh my God! Jack's father?" Rachel cries out, "We have to warn him!"

"No, we can't!"

I didn't mean to snap at her and regret my harshness in the same breath. More gently, though still unrelenting, I explain, "We can't take that chance. Jack might not become president. Who knows what would happen then. It's horrible, but we don't have a choice."

Rachel sees that I am steadfast on this point, and it causes her anxiety of the worst kind—the kind where you are forced to choose between something dreadful and something even worse. Tears well up in her eyes, conveying her unspoken words: "How can we let him die?"

The intensity of gut-wrenching sorrow is something that none of us can withstand indefinitely. It would kill us. Thus, self-preservation embedded in our DNA causes such anguish to diminish with time. There is no way to move forward otherwise.

I understand this natural progression and wait patiently. When the inevitable has found a place to settle in Rachel, she tries to make sense of it.

"Jack. President?"

I nod yes.

"He was president in my time. It was crazy then. We had a global pandemic and widespread depression. Social unrest wreaked havoc everywhere. I'm not sure Jack could have done anything differently. I'm not sure anyone could have. But the end result is that we go to war. The entire world goes to war. It's a disaster."

I can only imagine how bewildering it must be for her to hear all these things.

"And that is why the people, the people who sent you before, that is why they wanted him killed?" she asks.

"Yes. That's right. But it doesn't have to be that way. If Jack marries you, the future can change. You're smart, and he listens to you. I know every twist and turn in the road ahead. Together, we could point him in the right direction. A million people are bound to die."

I think a million deaths will hit Rachel the hardest. It doesn't. What she says next breaks my heart.

"You want me to marry Jack?"

Unable to meet her gaze, I look down and answer, "It's probably best for everyone." Then I realize…she knows when I'm lying.

Twenty-Eight

A gray, sullen day seems fitting for a funeral. Light rain cascades from the sky and I think, *Tears from heaven.*

Five hundred people from all walks of life have come to pay their respects to Sergeant Jonathan Campbell. Jack had no idea that his father touched so many lives, and it makes him question whether he really knew the man for all that he was.

There is not enough seating for everyone, leaving many to stand, huddled under their umbrellas. The ground is soggy, particularly in areas where the grass has not grown. Women with high heels have a hard time not sinking into the mud.

Family, friends, and fellow officers watch sadly as an American flag is draped over a simple pine coffin. A priest from the local church holds an open Bible and begins to read:

"The Lord is my shepherd; I shall not want. He maketh me to lie down in green pastures; he leadeth me beside the still waters. He restoreth my soul; he leadeth me in the paths of righteousness for his name's sake. Yea, though I walk through the valley of the shadow of death, I will fear no evil: for thou art with me; thy rod and thy staff they comfort me."

Jack consoles his mother, who is sobbing quietly. The rain has picked up, and he does his best to keep her dry with a large umbrella over them both.

Rachel, seated beside him, is protected by my umbrella held over her from the other side. She is not wearing any makeup, and the dark circles beneath her eyes show visibly.

Everyone is drenched in sorrow, but only I understand the extent of her torment. When I see her suffering like this, it is worse than pain of my own.

If I didn't know before, I know now. I will never stop caring for her. Nearby or from afar, I will watch over her. No matter what happens, she does not have to be mine for me to love her like she is.

The rain has gained momentum and beats down on tightly-held umbrellas. Undeterred by the downpour, officers in waterlogged uniforms stand united. Paul Nash, a thirty-year veteran of the force, has been selected to say a few words on their behalf.

"Sergeant Jonathan Campbell was my friend and hero. Time and time again, I saw him stand up for what was right, regardless of the risks to himself. He made a difference with his life, and we honor this great man. We all die. It is inevitable. But some of us, like Jonathan Campbell, live forever in our hearts."

Hearing the homage paid to his father affects Jack immensely—sowing the seeds of his interest in politics, just as it did before. Few will ever know that the most significant sacrifice made by Sergeant Jonathan Campbell had nothing to do with his job. He needed to die for his son to become president.

It is a tragic day for the Campbell family. Sadly, no other outcome was possible. If they could have only known that the wheels have already started turning for another event—one that will be celebrated by an entire nation.

Twenty-Nine

Eight hundred thousand people have come to witness the president of the United States being sworn in on the West Lawn of the US Capitol building in Washington, DC. It is a day ripe with optimism, where showmanship will merge with long-standing traditions.

Readings by renowned poets, music by famous artists, and prayers by religious leaders have been arranged so that there is something for everyone. Afterward, men in stately tuxedos and women in fancy gowns will dance the night away at the inaugural balls.

For the big day, Jack has chosen a navy suit, impeccably tailored and tastefully accentuated with a sky blue tie. Experts in public relations agree that navy is the color of trust and authority. They should have noted that it makes the future president appear quite handsome as well.

Jack Campbell would never have believed that many voted for him because of his good looks. The truth is, they did. With one hand up and one hand down on the Lincoln Bible, he proceeds to take the oath—as has been done by forty-four presidents before him.

"I do solemnly swear that I will faithfully execute the Office of President of the United States, and will to the best of my ability, preserve, protect, and defend the Constitution of the United States. So help me God."

Rachel, in a silk suit matching the color of Jack's tie, stands by his side. She has trimmed her long hair and wears it fashionably at shoulder length. Her style is simple, yet refined—a signature elegance soon to be emulated by designers of the day. It is only the Timex on her wrist that appears out of place.

Jack was embarrassed about the watch and offered to buy her something more expensive. She would not hear of it.

"This watch is to remember our times together," she reminded him.

What could he say to that?

From the campaign strategy to the details of his inaugural day, Jack Campbell has trusted his wife. Even his choice for vice president, critical to any presidency, was discussed with her beforehand.

Previously the governor of California, Gord Nelson is an elder statesman who brings valuable experience to one of the youngest presidents ever to be elected—a president the first to enter office without a military or public service background. Next to his second-in-command, the most powerful man in the free world looks almost boyish.

I am seated in the same row as Jack's mother, Rachel's parents, her brother, his wife, and their four children. It warms my heart to be treated like family.

As is the case with many immigrants, Mr. Lee came to America because he believed it was the land of opportunity. Even so, in his wildest dreams, he could never have imagined that his daughter would be first lady one day.

I, on the other hand, have known this was a moment in coming for some time. And yet, it feels surreal to me as well.

My closest friends are the epitome of an idyllic couple. *They look perfect together,* I tell myself...even as my stomach tightens into knots.

*****

Two weeks later, when the excitement has subsided, Jack arranges for us to have a private meeting. As soon as I enter his office, he rises to greet me with a brotherly embrace. "Good to see you!"

I'm touched by his warmth and pleased to see that, despite becoming president, Jack Campbell has not changed.

"Back in school, you passed me the ball. Looks like you haven't stopped doing that!" he says graciously.

I shake my head as if to indicate, *No—not really.*

"It would have been a tough election without your support. Can't thank you enough."

I did help him win, but there's no need to mention it.

"Got your back, Mr. President."

These words embody the comfort and familiarity of old times, and we both feel it.

"I can count on you, Bruce. That's why I want you to reconsider my offer. We could accomplish great things together. It would be amazing, don't you think? And, by the way, it's just me, Jack, not Mr. President. We've known each other too long for that."

Jack is extremely persuasive, and I'm flattered that he feels so strongly about having me join his administration—especially since there is no shortage of outstanding men and women who covet the opportunity. If it were possible, I would have gladly accepted.

"I'm no good with politics," I tell him sincerely. "You're better served with me in the private sector."

Jack is disappointed, though not as surprised as I thought he would be. He probably thinks I turned him down because I make more in a year than any politician could earn in a lifetime.

He's wrong about that.

"I can't change your mind?"

"No," I answer delicately.

"Even the president is no match for you," he says in good humor.

I'm remiss to let down my friend, but there was never a choice.

"You will be a great president," I tell him. It was always his destiny, and I'm grateful to have played a part.

With a full agenda and our business done, Jack rises from his seat to indicate that the meeting is over. As we walk toward the door, he pats me solidly on the back.

"And Rachel will be a great first lady. She's on the cover of every magazine. The press is having a field day!"

"Remember the Kennedys? It's the same excitement with you and Rachel."

My comment, unbeknownst to Jack, is factually based. On my payroll, there is a team dedicated to monitoring the chatter about the president and his wife. Public opinion can be fickle. I stay ahead of the curve.

Jack grins as if he were disclosing a secret. "She speaks Mandarin and Spanish too. I thought she was going into business, but she switched. Who knew! You can imagine how helpful that's going to be."

I nod to agree, remaining tight-lipped about Rachel's change of heart. In the role of first lady, being able to communicate without a translator is far more valuable than the ability to analyze income statements and balance sheets. Rachel, being who she is, planned ahead. These thoughts go through my mind as I leave Jack's office.

Secretly, I had hoped to see Rachel on this visit as well—and there she is, down the hall! She must have been waiting for the meeting to end.

The sight of her makes me happy in a way that I'm unable to explain. Nothing in the world has that effect on me. My entire physiology spontaneously changes.

She is the light through the break in the clouds, the light that makes me believe there is a heaven. Even if I wanted to, I couldn't change how I feel. It just is.

With a face full of hope, she asks, "Will the two of you be on the same team again?"

Working with Jack would give me proximity to the girl of my dreams. The thought is tempting beyond belief. Three, however, is an odd number...and untenable in a relationship.

"I'm better on the sidelines."

"I see," she says, blending disappointment with understanding.

So much has happened since high school, yet I remember sitting with her at the kitchen table as if it were yesterday.

Not now, I tell myself. *Let it go*.

"My turn to pass the ball?"

The resignation in her voice cuts into me. There is no point in acknowledging the obvious. We've come too far for veneer and platitude. I reach into my pocket and pull out a device half the size of a playing card.

"If you need anything, and I mean anything, anytime, anywhere, you can reach me with this."

She accepts the phone slowly.

"What will you do now?"

I think about how circular life can be.

"Looking to buy an island. Need to prepare."

She knows about the upcoming war.

"So soon?"

"Not raining when Noah built the ark."

I'm trying to sound clever, but my words ring hollow. The truth is, and has always been, I am adrift without her. I sail rudderless, without a destination. Beneath the rhetoric is a man grasping for purpose, a man desperate not to lose himself.

Her smile hints of regret, and it strikes me at the core. I want to throw my arms around her; I want to tell her that I have never stopped loving her; I want to say that a moment without her is an eternity. Instead, I stand there like an idiot…in dead silence.

We look into each other's eyes and, for an instant, it feels as if all that could not be said is understood. I drink in her presence as if I were returning to a desert—to a place where water may never be found again.

Even as I walk away, I know that part of me has stayed behind. It is, as it has always been… my heart belongs to her.

Thirty

I n 2025, when I am in my first year at West Point, President Campbell is in his first year of a second term. This time, Jack Campbell becomes president in 2016.

The first time, he marries Katherine St. Clair. Her father, a self-made billionaire, finances his son-in-law's campaign. This time, he marries Rachel Lee, and I use the full force of my wealth and social media empire to get behind the man destined to be president.

Most people believe their opinion of Jack Campbell was formed independently. They do not know that being methodically exposed to well-crafted stories about him over the years has shaped their thinking. Through the use of Facebook, Google, YouTube, and

Twitter—companies I control—Jack Campbell is a household name well before his election. Men and women alike think they drew the picture, when all they did was join the dots.

In retrospect, I was too effective.

I miscalculated.

I should have considered the impact Rachel would have as well.

People love that she is an immigrant. Even more so, they love the idea that anyone, regardless of his or her background, can ascend to the highest office in the land.

Jack and Rachel's humble origins are symbolic of the American dream, and they are embraced for it. Everyone cheers for *David*, not *Goliath*. Together, as a couple, they create an unstoppable momentum with Jack becoming president four years earlier than before.

I didn't count on that.

In my previous timeline, the war started in Jack's second term. If nothing changes, the war will now take place after Jack leaves office—too late for me to affect policy. The decisions I made for myself, for Rachel, for my parents, all thrown into question with this turn of events.

I can't help asking myself, *Was it worth giving up so much? Will it even matter?*

Trading a million lives for two makes no sense mathematically. That said, it is something I seriously considered. A million is a big, faceless number. My parents are...my parents. I could have disobeyed the general. I had time.

But if I made this one alteration, I would never have been sent back, I would never have met Rachel. If I had chosen to save my mother and father, the girl I love would have surely died.

Every simulation shows there are no outcomes without collateral damage. No matter what I do, someone else pays. All the money in the world is futile against such impossible choices.

Each day, I struggle to keep these demons at bay because spiraling into a dark abyss—for all the self-pity that it would absorb—helps no one. The only thing worse than letting my parents die would be for their deaths to be meaningless.

The message from the letter was clear: use your knowledge wisely.

So, I will myself to focus on the task at hand. Was it luck or destiny that I had a fascination with the stock market and had studied past cycles and the causes of them as a hobby? Hard to say, but nothing could have been more useful.

In the 1980s, the highest returns are found in Japan. This stock market is skyrocketing. Within a decade, an investment of $10,000 will be worth $100,000.

I ride this market as far as it will go. Then, in November 1989–just before the peak is reached—I load up on Nikkei puts. These options, betting that the Japanese market drops, cost pennies. Nobody believes it will happen.

When the Nikkei collapses a month later, not to return to its prior level for 30 years, I reap millions from an investment of thousands.

A similar opportunity arises in 2008, during the financial crisis. My position in credit default swaps turns into billions when the subprime market crashes through the floor. Whether the market is going up or down, I make money—lots of it.

Knowing that technology is the future, I parlay these gains into companies such as Amazon, Facebook, and Google. All my holdings generate massive returns, except for one. I own Moderna for other reasons.

Years from now, this company will develop a vaccine for Covid-19. Spending aggressively on R&D, I bring forward their discovery. A solution will be in place before the monster arrives.

Securing the vaccine, however, is only one part of the equation. People have to want it. None of it works without herd immunity. How can they be convinced?

I start by commissioning leaders in epidemiology to publish papers warning of an imminent pandemic. Armed with this research, Rachel convinces Jack to spearhead a campaign for the world to be vaccinated against a virus similar to SARS. In support of the president, the Bruce Meyer foundation provides these vaccines free of charge.

Averting a global pandemic might be just what it takes to thwart economic upheaval and social unrest. Cut off the roots of instability, and the war may never come to fruition. It's worth a shot.

As Tom Waites, I have lived through all of this before and remained silent—though I don't know how. The only consolation must have been that I would make it right the second time around...with the exception of my parents. Could I ever be forgiven for that?

There is, however, as if by providence, something that was overlooked by the general. In 1985, the year I am sent back, my parents are just six years old. This timeline allows me to watch them grow up, fall in love, have a son. I can partake of their lives and feel connected to them this way.

Flying in on my private jet, I visit the old neighborhood and re-experience my first bike ride behind the one-way glass of my Tesla.

My father holds the back of the bicycle and runs to give my younger self a start. When he lets go, I'm wobbly at first but adjust quickly. Feeling proud of myself, I turn my head to see if he is watching.

Despite all the years that have gone by, the expression on my father's face is exactly as I remember it to be. It is love, joy, and pride exquisitely intertwined. Seeing it play out again warms my heart and breaks it at the same time. He looks so young.

The next morning, I return to see my

mother walk her son to the school bus. She is holding my lunch bag, which contains a small heart cut out from tissue paper to remind me of her love through the day.

Seeing my parents from the eyes of a grown man does not diminish the yearning I have for them as if I were still that small boy.

You let them die!

You let them both die!

These thoughts condemn me without mercy. It is the reason I wake up screaming in the middle of the night. The guilt is never ending.

Rachel Lee

Thirty-One

On a rare night without a meeting, a function, or a pending issue, Jack and I relax with a game of chess after dinner. We enjoy watching the evening news and leave the television on while we play. Tonight they are discussing the economy, a topic that captures our attention.

"President Campbell is spending on infrastructure to fight unemployment."

"That's right. He's putting people back to work to fix bridges, roads, and airports."

"And we need that—so much of it is falling apart."

"Unemployment has fallen six months in a row."

"With the economy rebounding nicely, it's

no wonder the president's approval ratings are high. Americans agree, he's doing a fine job."

These words echo how proud I am of Jack. "Congratulations. Well done!"

He has a sparkle in his eye and leans in to tell me, "We both know you had a hand in this."

"Just being a supportive wife, Mr. President," I reply while thinking, *Bruce should get the credit.* Over the past three years, he was the one who provided the roadmap for Jack's policies.

A strong economy is like a rising tide that lifts all ships. It leaves most people better off. Naturally, they are pleased with the man in charge—even if they are unimpressed by his initiatives on health.

The president has single-handedly quashed the pandemic, yet it has gone largely unnoticed. No one is grateful to be saved from a catastrophe that never happens.

I wish I could tell Jack about the magnitude of his actions. It is his greatest achievement, and he deserves to know. I look at him fondly with words he will never hear.

He sends me a smile and turns his attention

back to the chessboard. After considering his options, he moves his bishop. It is a fatal error.

I position my castle decisively and confirm the play.

"Checkmate."

Jack touches his king—looking for an escape. There are none.

"Don't tell anyone the president loses to his wife in a game of strategy, okay?" he teases.

"Well, the queen is the most powerful piece for a reason," I say as if I were serious.

Jack chuckles, and it makes me admire him more. Only strong men lose gracefully.

Something else is on his mind.

"Have you heard from Bruce lately?"

We spoke yesterday, which I refrain from mentioning.

"He invited us to his island. You've just been so busy."

On the coffee table is a *Forbes* magazine, and I show it to Jack.

"He's on the cover this month. Richest man in the world."

Jack shakes his head.

"Remember when he told us he didn't know what he wanted to do?"

I nod yes. How could I forget? It was the last time we were all together...with Jack's father.

"Looks like he's getting by," Jack says amusingly.

"Barely," I reply, playing along.

Taunting me, he says, "And you settled for the president."

How do I answer that?

I smile and think, *You have no idea.*

"Let's do a quick visit," he suggests, "for the day."

I'm thrilled at the prospect and can hardly contain my excitement. Though I speak to Bruce regularly, I haven't seen him since the day he came to the White House.

"With the election, I could use his support," Jack says.

My heart sinks. Our trip is about money.

"Sure, I'll let him know."

There is no question in my mind that Bruce will give Jack whatever he wants.

"After I'm elected, we should go to Asia."

Jack speaks as if his second term were a done deal.

"Sounds good," I answer, doing my best to appear engaged.

He contemplates out loud, "India will be our first stop."

I nod to agree even though my mind has wandered elsewhere.

"Would be a watershed event if I could get the countries in this region to work together," he says enthusiastically.

Another four years will allow Jack to execute his global initiatives, and I tell him what he wants to hear, "You're going to make history, Mr. President!"

Without doubt, Jack is a visionary and I respect him greatly—even if I can't stop thinking, *I'm going to see Bruce!*

It has been a full day, and Jack is ready to call it a night.

"Ready for bed?"

"In a bit," I answer. Feeling restless, I need a few minutes to myself.

As Jack enters the bathroom, I walk over to the dressing table where I brush my hair each night. Seated on the upholstered stool, I peer into the mirror and ponder about the person I've become.

After Bruce told me that Jack was going to be president, I changed my plans to be more effective in the role of first lady. It was entirely my decision to study history and languages instead of finance and investments. But there are moments, like tonight, when it feels as if I've lost my way.

To be the first lady of the United States of America is a tremendous privilege, and I do not trivialize the position. It's just that this life was never my dream.

Some days, I feel like a sparrow in a golden cage. Nowhere can I be myself. Nowhere can I be free.

Turning to the jewelry box, I find the bracelet from Bruce. This keepsake is a familiar friend, and I pause before slipping it over my wrist.

Like a tidal wave, the past comes rushing at me, and I wonder…*What would my life have been with Bruce?*

Jack Campbell

Thirty-Two

On a rare night without a meeting, a function, or a pending issue, Rachel and I relax with a game of chess after dinner. The evening news is discussing my economic initiatives and we take a break to watch.

"President Campbell is spending on infrastructure to fight unemployment."

"That's right. He's putting people back to work to fix bridges, roads, and airports."

"And we need that—so much of it is falling apart."

"Unemployment has fallen six months in a row."

"With the economy rebounding nicely, it's no wonder the president's approval ratings are high. Americans agree, he's doing a fine job."

"Congratulations. Well done!" Rachel says to me.

"We both know you had a hand in this," I admit to her honestly.

"Just being a supportive wife, Mr. President," she replies sweetly.

It is an understatement because she has been invaluable to my career. I smile at her and turn my attention back to the game. There are a few options: none good. Choosing the cleanest shirt in the dirty laundry bin, I move my bishop.

Rachel places her castle in direct sight to my king. "Checkmate."

I look for a way out and realize, *She has me cornered!*

"Don't tell anyone the president loses to his wife in a game of strategy, okay?"

"Well, the queen is the most powerful piece for a reason," she points out.

I chuckle—there is truth to that comment. Preoccupied with my thoughts of the election, I didn't play well tonight. We need to start fundraising, and I know the person with the deepest pockets. It makes sense to go to there first.

"Have you heard from Bruce lately?" I ask. Over the years, Rachel has grown closer to him.

"He invited us to his island. You've just been so busy."

She reaches for a magazine on the coffee table and shows me that Bruce is on the cover of *Forbes*.

Richest man in the world? Really?

How did that happen?

I shake my head, "Remember when he told us he didn't know what he wanted to do?"

She nods yes, picturing that scene in her mind.

"Looks like he's getting by."

"Barely," she replies.

I press on, fully aware that she is humoring me.

"And you settled for the President."

She doesn't utter a word, but her loving eyes tell me everything. I am a lucky man.

"Let's do a quick visit," I suggest, "for the day."

Rachel's face lights up. She is just as excited to see Bruce as I am.

"With the election, I could use his support."

"Sure, I'll let him know," she says happily.

Asia is my priority in the next few years. A

tour of this region with Rachel by my side will capture the attention of the world. I tell her India will be our first stop, and I share with her my goal of increasing trade in this region.

The domestic economy was the focus of my first term. It will be the imprint I leave on the global stage that marks my leadership in the second. Rachel predicts I will make history, which is deeply gratifying. I think of my father and how proud he would be. Perhaps he is smiling down on me now.

With a meeting early in the morning, it's time to call it a night. I reach over to kiss Rachel on the cheek and ask if she's coming to bed.

"In a bit," she answers as I enter the bathroom.

While brushing my teeth, I remember a last-minute lunch with the ambassador of Canada and his wife tomorrow. Opening the bathroom door, I am about to ask Rachel of her availability when I see that she is staring at a colorful bracelet on her wrist. It looks to be a puerile trinket, and it perplexes me.

Where have I see it before?

My brain searches for an answer. Slowly, but then all at once, it dawns on me. She had it at the prom! I recall thinking how odd it was for her to wear something so childish.

Why is this bracelet significant?

Like the one snowflake that triggers an avalanche, Bruce comes to mind. The glances, the looks, the smiles—they fit the pattern of what I now know.

How could I have been such a fool!

I step back into the bathroom and close the door delicately. Leaning against the wall, I grind my teeth and shut my eyes...letting the immensity of this realization overtake my body. After a few minutes, when my blood doesn't feel like it's boiling anymore, I walk over to the toilet, flush, and count to three before coming out.

Climbing into bed, I look over at Rachel brushing her hair. And, just did like that, as with the slight twist of a kaleidoscope, everything is changed. Without another word, I turn my back to her and close my eyes—pretending that sleep will come easily.

In this instant, I want nothing to do with Bruce Meyer. But I need him to win, and that makes me hate him even more.

Bruce Meyer

Thirty-Three

I wait anxiously for the arrival of the president and first lady, who are simply Jack and Rachel to me. It has been raining for days, and I'm pleased that the weather—about the only thing beyond my control—has turned for the better.

Weeks ahead, the entire staff was prepped for an upcoming visit. None of them were told the identity of the guests, but they suspected that it must have been someone seriously important for me to ask about fresh flowers in the powder room.

When *Air Force One* touches down, and the door opens, Jack and Rachel step out into the sunlight. They pause on the platform to take in their surroundings and wave when they see me.

My staff thinks, *No wonder. It's the president!* They have no idea it is the first lady who takes my breath away.

In my mind, I have pictured Rachel a million times. None of it compares with seeing her here, in person. I feel the sun on my skin; I hear the melody of the birds; and I drink in the fragrance of the surrounding floral. All my senses are heightened with her presence.

Rachel looks as fresh as the first day of spring in a white dress with a pastel pink sweater—the same colors she wore at the prom. It has been a lifetime since high school. Yet, to me, it could have been yesterday. I greet them both with profound gratitude for our lasting bond.

Jack's sense of humor kicks in.

"Geez, Bruce, there's more security here than the White House."

"Important guests," I reply.

Rachel smiles at the flattery, and it mesmerizes me. Nothing is more beautiful than that smile. This visit is all that I've thought about since her call, and I can hardly wait to unveil my surprise.

"Come on. I have something to show you!"

A Land Rover, converted with a pop-up top,

awaits us on the runway. Jack and Rachel do not hesitate to travel this way—to the chagrin of their security detail.

We proceed through a fortified gate and enter a lush forest with elephants, giraffes, monkeys, horses, and countless other animals wandering freely. It might have been the garden of Eden.

Rachel marvels at the diversity, and I tell her, "Animal sanctuary."

"Oh, Bruce," she exclaims, "my dream!"

Keeping this project a secret was no easy task. So many times, I nearly relented. Seeing her light up, right beside me, I'm glad I didn't.

"Thanks, buddy. Now she's never coming back to the White House," Jack says in jest.

I chuckle at his comment and tell him, "There's no chance of that."

Rachel is spellbound by the animals. She looks like a child in a candy shop. Thinking back to all the years that she wrapped boxes of tissue, it feels like the world has unfolded as it should.

"This is incredible!" she squeals with delight.

Making her happy brings me more joy

than anything I could ever do for myself. Her dreams became mine…and I don't know when it happened.

Jack has remained uncharacteristically subdued. It's time to pay attention to him. "What can I do for you?"

He straightens up, clears his throat, and launches into his pitch.

"As you know, the election is coming up. Can we count on your support again?"

I don't need to think about backing my best friend. "Absolutely. One hundred percent. Anything you need."

Jack held out his hat, and it was filled to the brim. Clearly, he is pleased. With boundless funding and the reach of my social media empire, his prospects of remaining in office are just about guaranteed.

Rachel smiles awkwardly. I know she is uncomfortable with asking for money, even if all politicians do it.

Salaries, rent, travel, advertising, and more—expenses add up quickly in a campaign. I would gladly write a check every day of the week to see her but, truthfully, Jack has earned a second term in his own right.

"You've done a great job. People want you to remain in office. Your reelection is a slam dunk!" I tell him.

He catches the basketball reference and laughs lightly. We complete the tour of the sanctuary and return to the landing strip. Stepping down from the Land Rover, he shakes my hand.

"Thanks again. It feels like I've been to Fantasy Island."

Rachel winces at his remark.

"We have to get going though," Jack says, glancing down at his watch as if he were already late for an appointment.

Rachel had told me they were staying for the day and looks just as perplexed as I am by Jack's announcement.

"Something to eat before you go?" I suggest in an attempt to keep them longer. "We grow the vegetables ourselves."

"Next time," Jack answers tersely. His response reminds me of what parents say to their children for toys that will never be purchased.

"You're both my family. Welcome anytime."

In the back of my mind, I am thinking, *I have no one else*.

My instincts tell me there is something different about Jack Campbell. I just don't know what it is. Now, as I accompany my dearest friends back to *Air Force One*, I can't help wondering when I will see them again.

Jack is in a hurry and marches briskly up to the entrance of the plane. Rachel follows with a reluctance to her steps. At the top, they pause on the platform, where they stood merely a few hours ago—this time to wave goodbye.

Jack enters the plane first, expecting his wife to be right behind. Without warning, she turns around.

It is my moment of weakness, and she catches me pitifully unguarded. My eyes are tearful, my face is agonized, and I have nowhere to hide.

But this is Rachel—the girl who always responds with kindness. Magically, she kisses her hand and wills the wind to convey her affection.

Then, she is gone.

It leaves me broken and healed at the same time, and I stand there—fixated on the plane as it becomes smaller and smaller, until the dot that hints at its existence disappears completely.

How it is possible that I was on top of the world only moments ago?

Is misery from her absence the mirror image of euphoria in her presence? Does scarcity of water make it sweeter in the desert? Would it taste the same from the convenience of a kitchen faucet?

If I saw Rachel every day, would she become plain, ordinary, mundane? If there were no darkness, no pitch-black nothingness, could I conceptualize the presence of light?

Must extremes coexist?

I don't have the answers to these theoretical questions, and what difference would it make? My world will never be right without her. There is no point in trying to convince myself otherwise.

Having the time and solitude to contemplate what truly matters, I have come to the realization that none of it makes sense without the person you love.

If Rachel were in my life, I would treasure each and every moment. There would be no risk that I would take it for granted.

I hang my head low and kick away a single stone at my feet. These thoughts are delusional...I will never be with her.

Any trace of the white ribbon expelled by the exhaust of her plane is long gone when I look away from the sky. My driver has been waiting for me the entire time, and I wave him away. I am in no mood to speak to anyone.

Several hours later, on the road winding up to my house on the cliff, I am met by a breathtaking view. A canvas, awash with burgundy reds, brilliant yellows, and dazzling oranges, has been draped along the horizon. It is the spectacular farewell of a setting sun.

There would have been no greater joy than to have shared this splendor with Rachel. Conversely, there is no greater sorrow than to experience it on my own. As I open the front door and step over the threshold, I think to myself, *It is fitting that darkness will soon prevail.*

Once inside, I pass by the dining room. There, beautifully displayed, is a lavish feast of tropical fruits, assorted salads, grilled vegetables, T-bone steaks, and lobster. All wasted.

The kitchen staff, unsure of what to do, looks to me for guidance.

I shake my head and walk away.

Nobody says a thing.

They just witnessed something they did not know before: the richest man in the world can be let down.

Rachel Lee

Thirty-Four

Jack and I step out into the sunlight and a warm breeze brushes through my hair. Birds more colorful than the rainbow fly by, and flowers too beautiful for words bestow their gentle fragrance.

This is where Bruce lives?

This is paradise!

Upon seeing the boy who gave me his treasured bracelet, adrenaline surges through my body. I feel myself heating up and know that my face must flushed. Hopefully, no one else notices.

Jack jokes with Bruce about the amount of security on the island. It feels like old times with both of them laughing about it.

There is something that Bruce is anxious to

show us, and he leads Jack and me to a vehicle with an open top—similar to the kind used in safaris. Our security detail is not pleased about the arrangement, but they cede to Jack's wishes.

As we enter through a large gate and into a forested area, I am spellbound by what I see: elephants, giraffes, monkeys, horses, and countless other animals—all wandering freely!

Bruce engages me with an irresistible smile. "Animal sanctuary."

"Oh, Bruce," I cry out, "my dream!"

I can't believe he remembered what I shared with him all those years ago.

"Thanks, buddy. Now she's never coming back to the White House," Jack quips.

Bruce laughs at the harmless jab and tells him that there's no chance of that. Neither one of them knows what is going through my mind. To stay here, in this wondrous place, with Bruce...it all draws me in. Suppressing these thoughts, I compel myself to stay in the moment.

"This is incredible!"

Bruce has mischief in his eyes.

"Keeping it from you wasn't easy!"

I don't have the words to convey the depth

of my gratitude. This sanctuary means the world to me.

Bruce hasn't forgotten about Jack and turns his attention to him.

"What can I do for you?"

Jack clears his throat, "As you know, the election is coming up. Can we count on your support again?"

"Absolutely. One hundred percent. Anything you need," Bruce answers without hesitation, as I knew he would.

It is exactly what Jack came for, and he looks pleased. With Bruce on board, our funding issues are over.

I'm embarrassed that money is the real reason for the visit. Bruce, on the other hand, is not bothered by it in the least. He praises Jack effusively, telling him that his second term is a slam dunk.

The reference to basketball is clever and Jack appreciates it as well. As we come to the end of the tour, he thanks Bruce and remarks about how the place feels like Fantasy Island.

I'm aghast that Jack would say such a thing. He must not realize how insulting it sounds. I send Bruce a look of apology and am about to clarify the misunderstanding when Jack announces that we have to be on our way.

What? I don't understand. Our plans were to stay for the day. A meeting must have been added last minute. How I wish Jack had told me about it. This trip could have been rearranged. In any case, I am deeply disappointed.

"Something to eat before you go?" Bruce suggests. "We grow the vegetables ourselves."

This island and its sustainability is astonishing, and yet another reason to stay.

"Next time," Jack replies curtly. He makes eye contact with me and tilts his head slightly: let's go.

Every ounce of me resists, but I force a smile and follow Jack up the steps to the entrance of the plane. At the top, we pause on the platform where we stood only a few hours ago...this time to wave goodbye.

Jack enters first, expecting me to be right behind. I hesitate. The time with Bruce was so short. Succumbing to desire, I turn around for one last glimpse.

What I see is something I will never forget, something for which I am entirely unprepared.

Bruce looks frail, broken. His back is

slumped, his face agonized, and his eyes tearful. It is as if the seven-year-old boy I have always imagined is calling out to me.

Suddenly I realize, *I am not the only one who has sacrificed. He loves me! He loves me!*

Had I known how he felt before, would I have made a different decision?

No, I won't let myself go down that road. What might have been, what could have been, none of it matters now.

But, be that as it may, I'm desperate, so desperate, to abandon all and run to him.

Stop! Stop being so foolish! I scream without a sound. *You are not that girl in high school any more. You are the wife of the president of the United States!*

Duty and desire—like a tug of war— pull me in opposite directions. Yet, I know how it will end. The girl who is brave enough or selfish enough to choose what she wants is not me and never will be.

So, all alone on the platform, I do the one thing I can for Bruce. I kiss my hand and send a piece of my heart with the wind.

There is no choice.

I have to go.

Jack Campbell

Thirty-Five

For more casual meetings, I prefer the Rose Garden. It is a chance to be outdoors and to enjoy a breath of fresh air.

Today, I am seeing Katherine St. Clair, a classmate from law school. I remember her to be tall, with wavy red hair and a fair complexion.

Her father has the potential to be a large donor to the campaign, I tell myself, justifying a low-priority meeting on a busy day. Normally, a member of my staff would have sat in for me. But, feeling glum, I wanted the distraction. The trip to see Bruce was depressing. How did he become so successful?

After my presidency, I'll join a few boards, catch the lecture circuit, write a memoir. These things provide a decent living—nothing close to what he has already amassed.

Katherine rises to greet me, and I shake off my thoughts of Bruce.

"Wonderful to see you, Katy. You look lovely."

My memory has not done her justice; she is far more attractive than I recall.

"Thank you for seeing me, Mr. President," she says politely.

I think of our student days and keep it informal.

"Please, just Jack. It's not like we're strangers. Remember those marathon case studies?"

Reflecting on our past together brings a smile to her face, accentuating her high cheekbones.

"Now tell me, what's on your mind?"

"Mr. President..."

I look at her, bemused.

"Um...Jack," she corrects herself. "Do you realize that global warming threatens our very existence?"

With that bold statement, she reaches into her briefcase and pulls out a presentation complete with supporting charts and time-lapse photographs. It is impressive. She has done her homework and makes a strong case.

While I admire her passion for a worthy cause, it does not change the fact that our finances are stretched to the limit. Funding for new initiatives is just not possible, and I express my regrets.

"I understand, Mr. President..."

She pauses in mid-sentence.

"I mean, Jack. Sorry, I'm having trouble thinking of you as the president."

"I have that effect on people," I say half-seriously.

"No, no. I didn't mean it that way!"

She's flustered, and I find it endearing.

After being assured that no harm has been done, she smiles sweetly and picks up where she left off.

"You have budgetary constraints, I understand. But even the smallest steps in the right direction can make a difference. Letting people know it's a priority from the top, for example, would set the tone."

She might be right, I admit to myself. *Elevating awareness could be worthwhile*.

"Leave it with me," I tell her.

Katherine shakes my hand and looks at me shyly, "Thank you for the meeting...Jack."

I hear her words but only vaguely.

For some reason, I cannot take my eyes away from the luscious lips uttering those sentiments of appreciation. Why didn't I notice how beautiful she was before?

Subtly, I glance down at her left hand and observe—*no ring.*

"Would you like to have dinner next week?" It's not really a question because who refuses the president?

She looks at me oddly. The invitation has caught her off guard. Notwithstanding her initial reaction, she replies eagerly, "Yes, thank you. I would like that—very much."

Ray Sheldon, my personal secretary and the epitome of efficiency, suggests that we need to move on.

"Duty calls. Next week then," I tell her.

She smiles again and, for some reason, it strikes a chord with me this time. While walking away, I feel a sudden urge to turn around. And there it is! I see it!—the way that Rachel looks at Bruce—the way that no one has looked at me...until now.

"What night am I having dinner with her?" I ask Ray.

To my surprise, he reveals that I am fully booked and offers to send Katherine an apology.

"No," I say firmly. "I am having dinner with an old friend. Make it happen."

Devoid of emotion or judgment, he answers, "Yes, sir."

Katherine St. Clair captivates me, and I want to see her again. Why didn't I feel this way about her at Stanford?

I remember…

When I first met Katherine, my father had just passed away, and Rachel had changed her plans to be with me. Timing was bad.

It makes me wonder, *Would things have turned out differently if Rachel had gone to Columbia?*

Thirty Six

Patrons of Mazeta, an Italian restaurant with enviable reviews, will have to dine elsewhere tonight. Mario Mazeta knows that his regulars will be disappointed, but the chance to brag about a visit by the president could not be turned down.

For my "simple" night out, security is intense. Background checks are performed on every employee; walls and furniture are swept for wiretaps; and, as a fail-safe measure, bomb-sniffing dogs are deployed. What is said in this room stays in this room.

CAT, the Counter Assault Team, is charged with neutralizing the slightest threat. They have sharpshooters on the rooftops and multiple agents surrounding the area. For every man that is visible, there are ten who are not.

Five agents walk in tandem with me, forming a human shield. To be discreet, we will use the rear entrance. I pause briefly and straighten my jacket before entering through the back door.

Most people would find an empty room uncomfortable. For me, it is business as usual.

Katherine is seated at a table for two in a cozy nook by the fireplace. She looks content even though I have kept her waiting for over an hour. The meeting before ran longer than expected, and I was unable to excuse myself. Now, I can hardly wait to sit down with her.

There must be garlic bread in the oven, because the air is filled with a warm and inviting aroma. Red-checkered tablecloths imported from Italy; maple logs crackling in a wood-burning stove; and vanilla-scented candles glowing softly on the tables create a powerful ambiance.

This is not a meeting. This is a date.

I forgo the handshake and embrace Katherine like a long-lost friend. Her lovely face comes to life and delivers the smile that I've looked forward to seeing all day.

"I didn't know presidents could eat out," she says playfully.

"For good behavior," I answer with a grin.

From the start, the conversation flows like an easy river. We reminisce about our student days; we discuss the state of world affairs; and we are honest about the success and setbacks that have taken us to where we are today. There is no shortage of things for us to talk about.

The chemistry is undeniable. With each passing moment, I am more besotted by this fascinating woman, whom I never really knew.

"So great to see you, Jack," she says repeatedly.

I learn that she has followed my career each step of the way and maintains a file of my public appearances at her office. She knows every speech I have ever given as well. I had no idea. Her adoration is a fresh charge on an old battery.

"I still can't get over the fact that you're president," she tells me.

I frown at her comment.

"Oh no! I didn't mean it that way!"

She's alarmed until she sees that I'm not serious. Playing a prank on her takes me back to my youth. I haven't had so much fun in ages.

"Oh you!" she scolds harmlessly. "And to think I brought you a present."

She reaches down to a large bag at her feet, making me wonder what it could be.

As president, it is astonishing the kind of things I receive. At the White House, there is a room filled with vases, paintings, sculptures, and other discarded gifts. For political reasons, they are graciously accepted and stored away—never to be seen again.

"I know you're a fan," Katherine says with an official basketball in her hands.

"A big fan," I reiterate.

She rotates the ball to display the signatures of all the players and reads what they wrote: *"To President Jack Campbell, Hope you have a winning season."*

Basketball has a special place in my heart, and the Lakers are my favorite team.

"I love it! Thanks, Katy."

I reach across the table to kiss her on the cheek. She smiles at me with her entire being, and it melts the outer shell that is the president...leaving just me.

I don't know how it is possible to find her company soothing and exciting at the same time. Yet, it is precisely how I feel.

As the evening progresses, I find myself opening up to her in a way that I have not with anyone else...not even Rachel. Surprising myself, I share with her a premonition, a sense of foreboding, that I've had about the upcoming election.

"There's no need to worry, Jack. People love you!" Katherine says emphatically.

"Not everyone. I have enemies."

"All great men do."

Her comment is flattering and insightful at the same time, affecting me more than she could ever know.

"And don't forget the curse of the second term," I remind her.

"You're not superstitious?"

"I'm not. My mother-in-law is though. Told Rachel I should step down."

"That's crazy!"

"Yeah, good thing the press never got that."

"You're a born leader Jack, and you make your own future!"

Her unwavering support is the exact tonic for my ailment. In her presence, I am the man I want to be. I am enough.

"Did your father agree to this?" I ask while admiring the ball.

Now Katherine mocks being indignant.

"Hey, we both voted for you!"

She sees that I am not convinced.

"He owns the team, but all the players wanted to do it."

I look at this familiar ball and think of a time when I played the game that defined me for so many years.

"That would have been my dream..."

She looks at me curiously.

"So, you're just getting by as president then?"

Her words remind me of who I am—the wake-up call I needed! Realizing how ridiculous I sound, I look at her and burst out laughing. She joins in too.

Something marvelous happens when people laugh with each other, conscious or not. The world is lighter, happier, better. Laughter releases endorphins—that's the science—but all that matters to me is that I don't want the evening to end.

The candle on our table flickers with its last breaths. Where did the time go?

I reach for her hand under the table and whisper, "I'm having such a good time."

She blushes like a sixteen-year-old girl on a first date and gushes, "Me too."

We look into each other's eyes, overcome with an attraction that takes us to another world—a world where I am not the president—a world where I am just a guy who wants to see a girl again.

Suddenly aware of my indiscretion, I let go of her hand.

In the history of the United States, there have been presidents who had girlfriends while they were married. I never wanted to be one of them. Yet, here I am…in their shoes.

Did Katherine read my thoughts?

She lowers her voice and asks, "Can I interest you in a Lakers game? My father would love to meet you."

I want to see her again for any reason.

"Let's do it!

Katherine
St. Clair

Thirty-Seven

I can hardly believe that I am meeting with Jack Campbell, the president, even as I sit here waiting for him in the Rose Garden.

On the patio table in front of me is a tray with a pitcher of iced tea and some chocolate chip cookies neatly arranged in a row on a small plate. It makes me smile...these are the snacks Jack had when we studied together.

A server steps in to pour the tea for me, but just as I am about to take a sip, the president arrives with his security detail. I set my glass down and rise to greet him.

The president extends his hand to shake mine. "Wonderful to see you, Katy. You look lovely."

I had forgotten that Jack Campbell calls me

Katy. It's disarming. Only my father calls me that now.

"Thank you for seeing me, Mr. President," I reply politely. My voice is stiff and unnatural, because I'm so nervous!

"Please, just Jack. It's not like we're strangers. Remember those marathon case studies?" he says.

Of course I remember!

Jack would be surprised if he knew I've never stopped thinking about our times together. How could I forget those late nights in the study room: baggy sweatpants, cold pizza, and large cups of coffee to stay awake with the boy I so adored?

He is as handsome today as he was back then! The thought intrudes like an uninvited guest, and I'm thankful that no one else is aware of it.

All these years, I told myself that I was over him, that I'd moved on. Seeing him now, in person, I realize I am as smitten with Jack Campbell as I ever was. It is probably the reason I'm still single, even if I refuse to admit it.

"Now tell me, what's on your mind?" he says warmly, pulling me back to the present.

"Mr. President," I begin.

He gazes at me, and I realize my faux pas. "Umm…Jack."

I am the CEO of a multibillion-dollar corporation. How can a look from Jack Campbell reduce me to this? A bumbling idiot!

Shaking it off, I will myself to stay on point. "Do you realize that global warming threatens our very existence?" With that statement, I reach into my briefcase and pull out a presentation filled with charts and time-lapse photographs. My argument needs to be compelling.

"I care deeply about the same issues," he assures me. "There's just no room in the budget."

I see he is genuine, but I've come too far to let it go that easily.

"I understand, Mr. President—I mean, Jack. Sorry, I'm having trouble thinking of you as the president."

Did I just say that?

What is wrong with me!

"I have that effect on people," he says humbly.

"No, no. I didn't mean it that way!"

Could I be handling this any worse?

From the moment I was granted an audience

with President Jack Campbell, I rehearsed exactly what I would say. Now, dropping one ball after another, I'm no better than a second-rate juggler at a traveling circus.

Thankfully, he does not appear to be offended, and I continue with the purpose of my visit.

"You have budgetary constraints, I understand. But even the smallest steps in the right direction can make a difference. Letting people know it's a priority from the top, for example, would set the tone."

He nods to agree.

"Leave it with me."

It is a signal that the meeting is over, and I thank him for seeing me.

For a brief few minutes, I had the full attention of the president. There is nothing more I could have done. When I get back, I can tell my father I did my best.

Jack looks at me oddly, and I think he is going to wish me well.

That's not it.

Not at all.

"Would you like to have dinner next week?"

Really?

Did I hear that right?

My thoughts jump to the first day of law school, to the first time I met Jack Campbell. He took the seat next to me and defying logic or explanation, I found myself infatuated with him.

When we were placed in the same study group, I thought I'd won the lottery. It was while working on a case together that I summoned the courage to ask him out for a bite to eat.

"Thanks, but my girlfriend has dinner ready tonight," was a showstopper.

From then on, I was resigned to the fact that friendship was all I could expect from Jack Campbell.

Who could have known—after all these years—he would be asking me out?

A small voice inside my head insists on being heard: *he is married.*

I push it far away.

I am having dinner with the president!

No, correction, I am having dinner with Jack Campbell!

Rachel Lee

Thirty-Eight

The position of first lady is trickier than it appears. To be respected, I need to be distinguished in some activity. This activity, however, cannot be a conflict of interest with the president or one which could detract from him. Essentially, I am permitted to be successful, provided it does not matter politically or has the potential to overshadow my husband.

Such constraints rule out a career in business or finance, my areas of interest. At times, I envy Bruce—the freedom to do as he pleases.

In an interview at the beginning of Jack's term, I spoke of my decision to adopt a plant-based diet and intimated that it felt like a kinder and healthier choice. Within days, the Cattlemen's Association was up in arms, accusing me of causing injury to the beef industry.

This incident was deeply disturbing and a reminder of how careful I need to be with my comments. Perhaps it is the reason I started to write. Fictional characters can speak their mind without ramifications; they can suffer heartaches that could never be voiced. Stories allow me to hide in plain sight.

I wrote to escape. I did not think it would amount to much. Yet, our history is filled with the power of words, isn't it? People fall in love, unite for a cause, go to war—persuaded by words. It's all there in the chapters of mankind.

I did not envision such lofty goals. Nevertheless, it is wonderful when people read my stories.

Seated at the kitchen table, with a bowl of tomato soup, I contemplate the next chapter of my latest creation. Based on actual events at the height of the Second World War, I must do justice to the real heroes in this story.

Stirring my soup, I glance over at the empty chair where Jack usually sits to have dinner with me. He has been absent from many dinners recently and, in this moment of solitude, I find myself reflecting on our trip to see Bruce.

I may be physically present in the kitchen of the White House. My thoughts, however, have traveled back to that tropical island. What haunts me the most is the image of Bruce standing all alone on the runway.

You are married to the President of the United States, I remind myself sternly...but it is no use asking my head to overrule my heart.

Jack Campbell

Thirty-Nine

Tonight, the Los Angeles Lakers are up against the Toronto Raptors at the Staples Center. Expectations are high for the Lakers with many still remembering that Kobe Bryant scored 81 points against the Raptors in 2006. It was the second highest number of points scored in a single game and a personal high for him.

Having played seven NBA Finals at the Staples Center, the Lakers are under pressure to come through on their home turf. They have no idea that their fans are about to be treated to something totally unrelated to basketball.

The commentator, a master at what he does, ignites the crowd, "What a night, folks! You won't believe it! The president is here!"

Eighteen thousand men, women, and children erupt into cheers as I enter the stadium with an entourage of security. The jumbotron shows me, larger than life, shaking hands with everyone. Many in the stands know I'm a Lakers fan and identify with me this way. *Attending a game will enhance my popularity,* I tell myself.

Katherine and her father have a private box that seats thirty. Elegantly furnished, it reminds me of a suite at the Ritz. Lobster rolls, roast beef sandwiches, a Caesar salad, and chocolate chip cookies are offered on a buffet table for all to help themselves. In the fridge, there is a selection of wine and beer that would put most restaurants to shame.

Katherine greets me with a warm embrace. In a denim shirt paired with white pants and a turquoise necklace, she radiates a natural elegance. It is classy yet casual—not easy to pull off.

She introduces me to her father, a distinguished-looking gentleman in his seventies who could pass for ten years younger. During the flight, I was briefed on his background.

Kelvin St. Clair was raised by a woman who lost her husband before her last child was born. She scrapped to get by, but what she lacked financially, she made up with faith. From an early age, Kelvin was instilled with an unwavering moral compass. This internal fortitude, combined with the responsibility of looking after his mother and siblings from a young age, shapes Kelvin into a man who is independent, upstanding, and strong.

He is the epitome of what can happen when character, hard work, and good fortune all come together. Kelvin's untold wealth is entirely the result of his own making—a rages to riches story if ever there was one.

"Mr. President, it's an honor," he says with a sturdy handshake. If he is wondering why I am here with his daughter, he is not showing it.

"Please, just Jack, and the honor is mine," I reply earnestly.

Katherine smiles at me, and any doubts I had about flying in to see her dissipate into thin air.

Normally, I am captivated by a game with the Lakers. This evening, however, I want to be better acquainted with Kelvin.

"Katy tells me you were only twelve when you started delivering newspapers."

Kelvin notices that I just called his daughter Katy but doesn't skip a beat.

"I wanted to help out. My mother was left on her own and making ends meet wasn't easy."

"How did you do it? How did you build it all from scratch? It's so impressive. Your properties, your companies, the stadiums and, of course, the teams too. How?" I ask.

Kelvin is not one to belabor his success. "Well, I didn't know it was going to turn out that way. I bought a small building with my savings, fixed it up, and sold it for a profit. Just kept going from there."

"You make it sound so simple," I say while thinking, *There must be more.* In the presence of such humility, I am reminded that the great ones always make it look effortless.

"It's up to Katy now," Kelvin discloses, "I've stepped down."

I look over at Katherine and admire her modesty. You would never know she runs one of the largest private corporations in America.

Not one to squander an opportunity, Kelvin

changes the subject matter, "This is a great country. Dreams come true here."

I agree with a nod of my head to avoid disrupting his train of thought.

"The thing is, we're destroying the country, the planet, that has given us so much," Kelvin says with concern.

Five years ago, he and Katherine attended a World Wildlife presentation where they discovered that half of our animal species has been lost in the last forty years. At this meeting, they also learned that the increase in the acidity and temperature of our oceans has been destroying coral reefs and threatening all marine life.

Looking directly into my eyes, Kelvin asks, "What is progress if we decimate the world for it?"

Believing the answer to this question is self-evident, he presses on, "We've let this go too long already. Time is running out. Legislation to protect the environment is critical."

Katherine had told me that there was a time when her father was driven by the next deal, the next opportunity to grow his business. As a young girl, she would tour construction sites with him on the weekends. Back then, his focus was on the company, not the planet. Now, with fewer years ahead than behind, Kelvin cares deeply about issues beyond himself, issues for the greater good.

Do we feel the urgency of making a difference when the clock winds down? Perhaps, but Kelvin's steadfast conviction in right and wrong is admirable nevertheless. In him, I see my father.

"Dad, you promised. No politics."

"Yes, yes of course. Sorry about that," Kelvin concedes graciously to his daughter. "Let's just enjoy the game."

Katherine sends me a look of apology, and I smile back at her with no harm done. *Maybe they are right*, I think to myself, *I need to pay more attention to the environment.*

Rachel Lee

Forty

When I first started writing, I could not have imagined that my novels would be used in schools. It is a great honor, and I can't help wondering, *Was this my calling after all?*

Today, I am scheduled for a book reading at Woodward Elementary in Richmond, Virginia. Brooke Mitchell, my assistant; Frank Walsh, my bodyguard; and several other security personnel accompany me.

Brooke is a classmate from Stanford who followed me to the White House. Graduating at the top of her political science class and a recipient of the Dean's Award, she was, hands down, the most qualified for the job.

Then there is Frank, a Green Beret who would not hesitate to stand in front of a truck for me. His men in Iraq believed they would make it home because under the watch of Captain Frank Walsh, no man is left behind.

I am grateful for the devotion of these outstanding individuals. If escorting me to a school is trivial to them, they never show it.

Brooke can keep a secret, and I confide in her that visiting with students across the country means more to me than any of my other activities.

"Your stories are an inspiration to these kids. They see they have a choice in the person they become—just like the characters in your books. Is there anything more important than that?"

Brooke has a way of making people feel good about themselves. No wonder I enjoy her company.

As we enter through the double doors of the school gymnasium, we find ourselves met by a sea of cheering students. On display are paintings and miniature models made to depict various scenes from my novels.

I am overwhelmed by such a reception. In this moment, I know Brooke is right. Could I have done anything more gratifying?

My security team brings in boxes filled with books to hand out to the students, who are seated cross-legged on the floor. From their exuberance, you would think they were receiving a prize.

In the position of First Lady, I meet with world leaders, famous celebrities, and the list goes on. None of them have moved me as much as the look on the faces of these children.

Making eye contact with as many as possible, I address my audience, "Thank you for such a warm welcome. I am delighted to be with you here today at Woodward!"

Upon hearing the name of their school, the students let loose—clapping wildly until their teachers motion for them to stop.

In the center of the gym, a chair and microphone have been set up for me to be seen and heard from both sides of the room. I sit down, turn the book cover, and begin, "Courageous people are fearful like everyone else. They just act despite the fear."

After reading several passages, I pause and ask for questions. Most of the students are shy at first, but after a few have ventured forward, others join in and raise their hands eagerly.

I notice a boy, seated off on his own, oblivious to the discussion. He is looking down at his book, engrossed in reading. Later, his teacher casually mentions that she was surprised by his interest in my novel.

"Tony's a troublemaker and doesn't like to read."

"Thank you for telling me," I say, not letting on the monumental impact of her comment.

All along, I believed my writing was by chance—something I stumbled into accidentally. But what if that isn't true? What if I was meant to put a book into the hands of that child and the countless others I have yet to meet? The universe works in mysterious ways.

It makes me wonder…

The truth is, these students are a lifeline to me. Their outpour of enthusiasm and affection nourishes me like the sun and rain on a freshly planted field.

As we leave Woodward, I lower my voice to ask Brooke a sensitive question.

"In the past few months, the president has blocked off his calendar for personal reasons.

Can you let me know what they were for when we get back?"

Brooke understands what I am really asking. "Of course, ma'am."

Forty-One

It seems to me that loneliness is more intense at night. Perhaps the mélange of darkness and silence makes one feel solitude and emptiness more poignantly.

Tonight, like so other many nights, Jack is away. I rarely see him these days and when I do, he seems aloof.

Seated at my dressing table, I gaze into the mirror for an honest response. Staring back at me is a woman with soft lines around her eyes and strands of gray in her hair. The girl who married Jack Campbell has somehow disappeared.

How did it go by so quickly? How did I grow old, without realizing it?

There will never be a good time for what

I am about to do, so I resign myself to getting on with it. Lifting the lid of my jewelry box, I retrieve the bracelet from Bruce and set it aside. The communication device he gave me lies beneath, and I take it out. With the device in hand, I walk across the room and climb into bed. Leaning against two pillows fluffed up for back support, I pull the blanket up around me, feeling a sudden chill. It is not a call I want to make, but I need to know.

My fingerprint is instantly recognized, and I hear a familiar voice, "Rachel?"

Every room in Bruce's mansion has the ability to connect with this device, allowing him to answer on the first ring.

"Hi, Bruce. I hope I'm not calling too late."

"Never. It's good to talk to you any time. Are you okay?"

Fearful of losing my resolve, I dispense with pleasantries and get straight to the point, "I need to ask you something."

"Of course," he replies, without letting on that he hears the strain in my voice.

"Who was first lady? You know, when Jack was president before."

The question is straightforward, yet he hesitates—adding to my trepidation.

"Katherine St. Clair."

"Oh my God! Jack was supposed to marry her! Not me!"

It was a challenge but, with some digging, Brooke was able to discover that Jack has been seeing Katherine on a regular basis.

"She's the one who helped him get elected before, isn't she?"

"Yes, her and her father."

Bruce knows the information will be hurtful, but he owes me the truth.

"I'm sorry, Rachel. I'm so sorry," he says repeatedly.

As upset as I am, I can't help thinking, *Is it really Jack's fault?*

My head is throbbing. The voices won't stop, the voices that haunt me relentlessly: "You deserve this. You let his father die."

"How can I be mad at him?" I say with resignation, "I'm the one who changed his future."

"It's my mistake," Bruce insists. "Jack is president four years earlier than before. I didn't expect that, or Katherine."

Suddenly I realize, *Bruce already knew!* He was not fazed in the least. Was he protecting me?

I could blame Bruce…it would be easier, but I can't do it. Ultimately, it was my decision to marry Jack, wasn't it?

The photo on my night table beckons me, and I pick it up. In the picture, Jack is being sworn in as president with me by his side. My hand trembles and the image blurs so that it is Katherine who is standing in my place. I shake my head, forcing my eyes to see the photo as it is—with Jack and myself.

"I have to tell him."

"You can't, Rachel. Please, you can't. Think what it would do to him."

Bruce is trying to reason with me, and I have to admit…he's right. How could Jack ever accept that his life, his accomplishments, his marriage were all orchestrated? And, if he did, wouldn't he feel betrayed by his wife and his best friend?

No. Nothing good can come from going down that path.

But what to do now?

Why were Bruce and I so arrogant as to believe we could alter destiny?

Forty-Two

It is startling how you can know someone for years, be married to them even, and then find yourself wondering who they are one day. Somehow, a stranger has taken over the body of the person you use to know.

Sitting across from Jack at breakfast, I can't help thinking, *What happened to us?*

"Didn't know you had another dinner last night," I mention while digging into my grapefruit.

Jack sips his coffee. He has no intention of answering which forces me to continue.

"It wasn't on the calendar."

"Just seeing an old friend," he says dismissively.

I'm still working on the grapefruit and ask, "Anyone I know?"

Jack cuts into his omelet.

"No, not really. Not important."

He is unfettered by my question, and I think, *When did you become such a good liar?*

Putting down my spoon, I proceed with a deliberate course of action.

"Can we be honest with each other?"

Jack finishes chewing, swallows a mouthful of eggs, and comes back with a simple, "Sure." He was hunched over his plate but straightens up to show he is paying attention.

"I know about Katherine," I state plainly.

Jack lets go of his fork, looks me straight in the eye, and launches into a cover-up story. I could let him ramble on, but what would be the point?

Interrupting him, I say, "It's okay."

Unsure of where this conversation is headed, he leans back and waits for me to continue.

"I understand," I tell him, my voice quivering as I speak. I hate that. I thought I would be stronger.

Jack must have known his relationship with

Katherine ran the risk of being discovered. These things are hard to hide when you're the president and constantly watched. Still, he was willing to take that chance.

"I'm sorry. Didn't mean to hurt you."

Jack is sincere, I see that, and it makes all the difference.

In the movie *Love Story*, Ali MacGraw portrays a beautiful young woman who tells her boyfriend, "Love means never having to say you're sorry." I like her as an actress, but this line makes no sense.

Without a sincere apology, conflicts stack on top of one another, becoming mountains of resentment too steep for any relationship to overcome. *Sorry* is needed for a fresh start.

Jack's willingness to admit fault clears the way for me to ask the next question, "Do you love her?"

He stalls, not because he is uncertain. He is contemplating the repercussions of his response. I know this to be true because when he finally answers, "Yes," it is with conviction.

I flinch.

"Why?"

This time, Jack does not waver.

"She looks at me the way you look at Bruce."

I almost fall off my chair. The wind has been knocked out of me, and I can't breathe. What shocks me the most is the swiftness of his reply. How long has he felt this way?

My first instinct is to protest: "Bruce and I don't have a relationship!" But would that be the truth? Is desire to commit a crime the same as committing the crime?

In our legal system, the answer is a resounding *No!* Nevertheless, what if the bond between two people is so profound, so powerful that words and actions are unnecessary? Would that intimacy, would that be the betrayal?

If so, then yes, I am guilty.

The candor between Jack and me exposes our secrets to the light of day, and it lessens our burden. On the flip side, we have opened Pandora's box. There is no going back.

"I guess you can't help who you love."

It is the truth and the only thing I can think of to say.

"I guess not," he echoes back.

Jack doesn't mean to sound flippant, but it comes across that way.

"What do we do now?"

"Nothing, it's too close to the election."

"I don't think I can live like this," I say uneasily.

"You'll have to," he tells me while walking away—confident I won't strike back when wounded.

There will be no scandal.

Forty-Three

Left alone at the kitchen table with my half-eaten grapefruit, I stare into space and, unexpectedly, think of Brooke.

Brooke—beautiful, kind, clever—is a clear catch for anyone. Yet, most nights, she can be found alone in her apartment.

Does Brooke want to be married?

Yes, absolutely yes.

She wants that...and so much more. A three-bedroom bungalow, two children, a perennial garden, and a miniature pug are all on her wish list.

The problem is, Brooke is involved with a married man—a man who claims to love her even though he won't divorce his wife. Brooke has been with him since we were both at

Stanford and the excuses have remained the same.

"He loves me. He really does. It's just that he can't leave her."

"You deserve better!" I've told her many times. But now I think, *What do I know?*

The image of Bruce standing alone on the runway comes to me, and I realize that it is pointless to judge anyone or anything.

Everyone has a story.

Everyone has a reason.

Suddenly, these thoughts overwhelm me like a relentless rain that has, at last, seeped through all the layers of my clothing; and I begin to cry. Cupping my hands over my face, I sob uncontrollably.

I feel so sad, so desperately sad, not just for myself, but for Brooke and all the other Brookes out there.

Why do we do this to ourselves? Why do we love someone we can never be with?

Forty-Four

History shows that when the economy is robust, people vote for the incumbent. No one rocks the boat when times are good. And so, with policies that have kept unemployment low and the country vibrant, Jack Campbell is reelected by a landslide.

Our first trip overseas is to Asia, just as he envisioned. *Air Force One* takes us to Sardar Vallabhbhai Patel International Airport in Ahmedabad. Prime Minister Narendra Modi and his wife await us on the red carpet, rolled out for our arrival.

School children wave masks painted with the face of the american president, which they made in class. Dancers in bright costumes and musicians, including drummers and trumpeters, perform as if the festivities were to celebrate a national holiday. It is the first time that both the president and the first lady are visiting India, and we are being treated like royalty.

From the airport, we head to Motera Stadium, the largest cricket forum in the world with a seating capacity of 110,000 spectators. It is estimated that over six million men, women, and children have lined the streets along this 13.7 mile drive to catch a glimpse of us. The exhilaration in the air makes it feel more like a rock concert than a political gathering.

Through the five-inch bulletproof windows of *Cadillac One*, Jack and I wave at the crowds who have waited tirelessly. To the outside world, we have it all—high school sweethearts sharing the ultimate dream. Universally, we are an admired couple, and it makes me think of all those people who everyone believes are happily married…right up to the moment of their divorce.

In the privacy of our vehicle, Jack criticizes me for the smallest of things: my choice of dress, the way I did my hair, the color of my lipstick; and I know, *He does not love me anymore*.

I am saddened by this loss, but it sets me free at the same time...free of the guilt that I never truly loved him in return.

I realize now that a relationship can die fast or slow. Fast is mercurial and decisive. Accusations fly with heated exchange. Someone was wronged no doubt. The bridge has collapsed, and the river can no longer be crossed. There is nothing left to salvage.

Slow, by contrast, is far more subtle though every bit as lethal. While the bridge still stands, neither one has any desire to walk over it. Both gaze at each other from across the riverbank and wonder how they ended up so far apart.

If I had a choice, I would choose the first. Death by a single blow rather than a thousand tiny gashes. But, alas, it is not up to me. Jack and I are together yet apart. I suppose it has always been this way.

Our trip is heavily covered by the media and, despite the gulf between us, I am resigned to fulfilling my role as the president's dutiful wife.

When we arrive at our destination, Jack sends me a smile. I smile back. It is an acknowledgment of mutual respect and understanding. He loves Katherine and I, well, I suppose it has been Bruce in my heart all along. We are both prisoners of our own volition and, in that strange way, have empathy for each other.

Jack approaches Prime Minister Modi for their symbolic handshake. This image will be at the forefront of every news feed in the world, and the two of them conjure up their desired personas. Photographers jostle each other to capture the optimal angle for this symbolic act of friendship.

Without warning, one of the Indian bodyguards shoots Jack in the head and turns the gun on himself.

All hell breaks loose.

"Jack!" I cry out, my screams drowned in a sea of pandemonium.

I run to him, but Frank, my bodyguard, holds me back. Secret Service agents immediately form a perimeter around the president. The mayhem, the madness, I can't believe it is happening again—just like the prom.

Medics lift Jack onto a stretcher and hasten to an ambulance, which speeds away. In the frenzy, I'm almost knocked over. Frank takes a hold of me, using his body as a shield. He moves methodically, the calm in the storm.

"We have to go," he says, guiding me firmly into a limousine. Once inside, he asks, "Are you okay?"

I nod yes, but I'm not okay—not in the least. Jack, splattered with blood, is plastered in my mind. I can't stop shaking.

Frank takes control of the situation and instructs our driver to rush to the hospital. On the radio, reporters recount the biggest news story of their lifetime.

"Oh my God! The president of the United States has been shot. He is being rushed to the hospital at this very moment. We do not know his condition. I repeat, the president has been shot."

"I can't believe I just witnessed the president of the United States shot at close range. We will keep you informed of his status as soon as any information becomes available. Pray for now."

Forty-Five

nside the White House, the vice president of the United States is being sworn into office. The nation will be in good hands with Gord Nelson—though he never wanted to become president this way.

Air Force One brings us home.

It is a sad voyage that began with such promise. Jack Campbell returns to his country in a casket carried by men who are remorseful to have let him down.

I descend from the steps of the plane, gripping the rail for balance. Photographers will want images of the president's widow, and I hide my haggard appearance behind dark sunglasses.

Black limousines and a dreaded hearse

await us on the runway. Security is intense, but it is like applying a heavy dose of sunscreen after you've been burned. Frank never leaves my side and helps me into the back of one of these vehicles.

The communication device from Bruce vibrates inside my purse. I take it out and see his message: *Are you okay?*

They killed him. Right in front of me, I text back. My fingers quiver so badly that none of it would have made sense without autocorrection. As the first lady, I've had to put on a strong front, and it has been exhausting. With Bruce, I can finally let my guard down.

Be there soon shows up on my screen, telling me Bruce is on his way.

I tuck the device back into my purse and notice the face of my Timex is shattered. It must have happened in the chaos when Jack was shot. I don't know why I didn't see it before.

I stare at the hands of time, frozen in that horrid moment, and I remove the watch from my wrist. It is not how I will remember Jack Campbell.

These past days have been a blur.

Can he really be gone?

Recounting the dreadful events in my mind, I suddenly realize the courage of the man seated next to me. Frank Walsh never hesitated, not for a second, to make sure I was safe—even at his own expense.

I turn to him and say, "I'm sorry. I never thanked you."

Taking his hand into both of mine, I tell him what is long overdue, "Thank you."

"Just doing my job, ma'am," Frank answers, without belaboring his selfless devotion.

He has a family. How would they feel if he didn't come home? It makes me think of the sacrifices made by so many who serve our country.

Frank Walsh

Forty-Six

In 1961, President John F. Kennedy authorized the Green Beret headdress for the exclusive use of the US Special Forces. He called the Green Beret "a symbol of excellence, a badge of courage, a mark of distinction in the fight for freedom," and I am proud to have been part of that world...once.

Being a personal bodyguard is less challenging than my previous work. No question. But I have reasons for what I do.

When President Campbell was shot, my priority was to ensure the safety of the first lady. It is not that I am disloyal to the president. My mission is to protect her.

While on our way to the White House, I am taken aback by the depth of her gratitude.

With everything she has been through, I did not expect her to think of me.

In keeping with my training and protocol, I tell her I was only doing my job. Without question, I would have taken a bullet for the first lady—just not for the reasons she may think.

Six years ago, Matty, my two-year-old son, was diagnosed with a rare cancer. Doctors told my wife and me that five months was all we had left with our only child. There was, however, a specialist in Switzerland who might be able to help.

But Switzerland?

And the medical costs?

It might as well have been the moon for what a military man could afford.

All that changed when Bruce Meyer found out about our predicament. He paid the bills and had his private jet fly us across the ocean.

Today, Matty is in grade three—a happy, healthy boy with a faint scar on the left side of his temple.

There is nothing, *nothing*, that I would not do for Bruce Meyer.

Katherine
St. Clair

Forty-Seven

I have not left my penthouse in the past week. Curled up on the Poltrona Frau Kennedee sofa in my living room, I cannot take my eyes away from the 80-inch screen across from me. The teak coffee table is where I've been tossing my tissues and now, as I blow my nose, another will be added to the pile.

It feels like the bullet that ended Jack Campbell's life passed through me as well.

Nothing makes sense. Nothing matters anymore.

Ten years ago, when I started working with my father, I was determined to prove myself. It was important for me to demonstrate that I deserved the position, even if I was the owner's daughter. That meant weekends at my desk and showing up when I was sick.

How could I have thought anything was that important?

Days ago, I stopped going to the office, telling my father that I needed time off—uncertain of when I would return, if at all. He must wonder about the relationship I had with the president.

What can I say? There are no words.

My eyes are so red and swollen from crying that it hurts to blink. On the table beside me is a half cup of coffee and a frozen dinner that has dried out.

I cling onto the news, unable to let go of the only man I have ever loved. Hearing the details of his assassination, recounted over and over again, is pure torture. Yet, I cannot bring myself to stop.

In my grief, I am not alone. The number of viewers for the president's funeral is overwhelming—exceeding that of his inauguration. Even those who did not vote for Jack Campbell feel a connection to him now. Taken young and at the height of his popularity, he is a president who will be immortalized.

If Marilyn Monroe had left the world, withered and old, would she have attained iconic status? No, not likely. Just as she is frozen in our minds as a voluptuous, beautiful woman, so too will Jack Campbell be forever remembered as a great and flawless leader.

MSNBC, opportunistic to the public's insatiable appetite for anything to do with their president, follows the funeral coverage with a feature story about his personal life.

Brian Bradshaw, a highly acclaimed journalist, paints an idyllic portrait of Jack Campbell: his father was a law enforcement officer who lost his life in the line of duty; he took his high school basketball team to the state championship; he graduated in the top quartile of his law class; and it goes on. In sync with the commentary, video clips and photographs of Jack through the years are shown one after another.

Julie Rose, the co-anchor, builds on the narrative with a discussion about the president's fairy-tale romance. She speaks at length about how it was a dream come true for Jack Campbell to marry his high school sweetheart.

"No! No! No!" I shout wildly at the screen

Brian concludes by saying, "President Campbell was perhaps the most beloved of all presidents—leading America to enjoy the greatest prosperity it has ever seen."

Julie is compelled to add, "We will miss this great man." She is a seasoned broadcaster but tears up with those final words.

In these last few days, my entire world has imploded. Jack and I had so many plans after his presidency. He was going to marry me. We were going to start a new life together. The pain is unbearable and unending.

No one will ever know how much I loved Jack Campbell and he, me.

Rachel Lee

Forty-Eight

Citizens across America, in the cities, in the countryside, in their living rooms, in their kitchens, at work, at school, all stop what they are doing to watch the news coverage of the president's assassination.

The angst of an entire nation can be felt in the streets. Emotions range from despair to hysteria. Not since the assassination of President John F. Kennedy has the country mourned so deeply.

Journalists and political scientists discuss the turmoil that will now embroil the rest of the world. People, years from now, will remember exactly what they were doing when they heard that President Campbell was shot. It is one of those historic moments.

Across the nation, the American flag flies at half-staff. Out of respect, President Nelson orders the closure of all federal departments, agencies, and buildings.

Military guards from each branch of the United States Armed Forces carry the president's casket into the library of the White House. General Emmerson, the commanding general of the Joint Force Headquarters National Capital Region, acts as my escort.

At the family service, I slide my arm through my mother-in-law's, providing both physical and emotional support. I have lost a husband, but the other Mrs. Campbell has suffered the loss of a husband and a son. It must be unbearable for her. You're not supposed to outlive your child.

After the private service, we open the doors of the library to the public. The line of people waiting to pay their respects to the president is unending, with five thousand passing through each hour. Washington Metro subway will set a record for ridership this day.

Thirty-six hours later, as per his own wishes, Jack is flown to San Francisco, where he is to be buried alongside his father. Fighter jets fly in missing-man formation, and a twenty-one-gun salute honors the president who lies in a coffin with an American flag draped over it.

It feels like déjà vu as I stand where Jonathan Campbell and, now, his son are laid to rest.

I failed them both.

If only there was something, anything, I could do to make it right. Sadly, no such thing exists. Death is heartless that way.

Forty-Nine

An impressive helicopter has been given special permission to land on the lawn of the White House. It is Bruce Meyer, and he has come for me...having persevered for two lifetimes.

I see his silhouette in the distance. He is holding back, waiting patiently. There are many eyes on us, and he is being considerate of my reputation.

I reflect on my time with Jack and realize I was wrong. I did love him—just differently than how I love Bruce.

Is it disloyal to strive for happiness given everything that has happened?

It feels that way, and yet I want to be happy again.

With Brooke and Frank by my side, I address, for the last time, the people who have supported our administration.

"Thank you for helping me," I correct myself, "for helping Jack and me."

This life, this life as first lady, has come to an end; and I speak from my heart.

"Our paths may never cross again, but you should know how much your service has meant to me, to us. We are forever indebted to all of you."

I didn't realize that I would become so emotional in delivering this message. During our stay, the members of my staff have been like family to me. Holding back my tears, I wave goodbye.

My final act as first lady is to hand Brooke a sealed envelope addressed to a woman I have never met. Enclosed is a handwritten note with three simple words: *He loved you.* I owe Katherine St. Clair that much.

"This is a private matter. Can you make sure she receives it personally?"

"Absolutely, ma'am," Brooke replies.

I thank her, knowing that I have been blessed with a true friendship.

"It has been an honor and a privilege to serve you," she tells me. Her future with the new first lady is uncertain, yet she smiles courageously—a testament of her gentle strength.

I hold onto Brooke as if I were losing a sister and hope that she listens to my last words, "Take care of yourself."

As I walk toward the helicopter, I'm surprised to find Frank Walsh still accompanying me. I turn to him and softly say, "Thank you. I'm fine now."

Frank is polite as always, "Ma'am, I answer to Mr. Meyer. He placed me in the Secret Service to ensure your safety at all times."

Of course! Why didn't I think of it before? Frank is always there—always ready to stand in the way of harm for me.

I look at Bruce and know I am where I belong. No one loves me the way he does.

Bruce Meyer

Fifty

Rachel makes her way toward me, and it takes all my strength and willpower to show restraint. There is gossip about her decision to leave Washington, and I do not want to add to the speculation.

As I help her into the helicopter, the colorful bracelet on her wrist catches my eye. My heart skips a beat—just as it did the first time I saw her wearing it. The past and the future have come full circle.

"So sorry, Rachel."

She nods sadly.

"I know. Not your fault."

"You'll be safe," I assure her. "I have taken every precaution."

She looks up at me.

"How long before it begins?"

I don't have an answer for her.

It's different this time.

The war I knew was precipitated by a global pandemic, a financial crisis, and a wave of social unrest. These issues have been averted... at least for now.

"I'm not afraid. Whatever happens, I'll be with you," she says bravely.

I hold onto her hand, fearful that if I let go, she will disappear. To be with her, my soulmate, for the rest of my life—it is enough. No amount of money can buy me more time, but I do not resent that.

What is most precious of all should be granted equally. Twenty-four hours a day, 365 days a year—the same for the rich as the poor—to spend as we so choose. I will not squander a minute of it.

Is there a war on the horizon?

Possibly.

Regardless, someone else will have to navigate through those murky waters. I am not the captain of that ship any more.

We honor our heroes with statues because, somehow, we believe it will immortalize them.

In reality, people go about their day, walking past monuments without a fleeting thought about their significance.

Our lives are spent building castles in the sand. Large or small, grandiose or simple, it is inconsequential—all washed away when the tide comes in.

Nothing lasts. Nothing endures.

To love and be loved, it is the only thing that is real, the only thing that matters to me now.

I look at Rachel, and the young girl I met in the school cafeteria appears before me. Time has no impact when your eyes see through the lens of your heart. I will not give her up again, no matter the cost.

Every detail with Rachel is etched into my mind—how she carried my bag, welcomed me into her home, kissed me for the first time—and I know that I am done with duty and obligation.

If someone offered me a deal right now to bring Jack back for giving her up, I would not take it. It is not something I am proud of, but it is the truth.

Am I being selfish?

Perhaps, but I would gladly die for her in an instant. So maybe, maybe love is both. Maybe it is being selfish and unselfish at the same time. We are wired for self-preservation and, in the end, that is what it is...the most basic of all needs. I am not alive without her. I love her beyond reason, beyond comprehension; and she loves me.

That is all I need.

That is all I ever wanted.

When I think about the precious time remaining with Rachel, I regret that so much sacrifice was pointless. No man has the power to change destiny. What will happen will happen. The best we can hope for is to know love, truly and deeply. That is the heaven that is on earth.

The helicopter changes direction in midair and flies toward my island in the distance. Below, the ocean glistens from sunlight caught on the crests of its waves. The sky is a clear, wishful blue.

It is a beautiful day for a new beginning.

What's meant to be will always find a way.
—Trisha Yearwood

About the Author

I never thought I would be a writer.

My parents were immigrants who arrived in Canada with a dictionary and $200 in their pockets. For them, the fear of not making the rent or putting food on the table was constant. Understandably, financial security was a top priority.

Thus, I was encouraged to be a doctor, lawyer, or accountant—the emphasis on doctor. People get sick; it's a safe profession. Such was their reasoning, and I wanted to please.

Medicine, however, just didn't take for me. My brother, on the other hand, was a natural. He took one for the team and became an excellent physician, while I ventured into the investment industry.

After 30 years in this field and a multitude of market cycles, I realized that my experiences would be more of the same going forward. I enjoyed my time in the business. It just felt like there was something else I had to do.

Then, I happened to see a documentary about a Polish mother and daughter who hid Jewish families and a German soldier during the second world war. I was blown away. These women, through wit and courage, saved so many lives. Their choice to be kind in the face of unspeakable atrocities was more than inspiring. Surely, a book should be written about their story.

I never thought the author would be me, but that is exactly what happened. *My Mother's Secret*, published by Penguin Random House, became an international bestselling novel.

This time around, I woke up in the middle of the night with a dream that was as vivid as if I had just been to the movies.

I started writing again.

The result: *It Was Always Her.*

In this novel, I drew from my own background to develop Rachel's character and that of her family. Writing this story brought back so many memories...the most poignant being those of my parents.

I remember that when we first came to Canada, my father was anxious to earn a living. He took any job to make ends meet, but he was not a painter, a sheet metal worker, or whatever else he claimed to be. My father—a proud man—would be let go within weeks, if not days; and the search for work would begin all over again.

I can only imagine how stressful that must have been for him. A few years ago, he told me that one of the happiest days of his life was when he was finally hired as an aircraft mechanic—his true vocation—by Air Canada. He would work at this airline until his retirement and receive the *Award of Excellence* for exemplary service.

My mother was exceptional in her own right. She was a kindergarten teacher who had no prior experience with a sewing machine. Even so, she would go on to become the best seamstress at the factory where she worked—setting records for productivity that no one else could match. She also did piecework for extra money and, like Rachel, I helped her each night.

My mother would end up buying the factory where she started out by making $40 a week.

You may wonder why I would include my parents in the section about the author. Quite simply, it is because there is no author—there is no me—without them.

Each step of the way, every journey I have taken, they were there. Through their example, they showed me the way and shaped me into who I am…and want to be.

Now, back to the story.

In grade four, as with Rachel, I came up with 250 words to win the contest. The teacher did not believe it possible and scrutinized my work.

I don't know why such a trivial incident has stayed with me all these years…except that I was just so proud of myself.

Rachel's school visit is also taken from a personal experience. In the gymnasium where I was giving a book talk, the walls were decorated with posters created by the students to welcome me. Also on display were models, made from plasticine and cardboard, to replicate scenes from *My Mother's Secret.*

In my previous job, I met with political leaders and the senior managements of major corporations around the world. It was a privilege to have had such access but, the truth is, none of it compares with meeting these children. To this day, I see the smiles on their bright-eyed faces as clearly as if it were yesterday. It is a gift I cherish and a memory I will never forget.

At another school, there was a boy who finished reading *My Mother's Secret*, even though he didn't like books. His teacher found it surprising and thought I should know. Her words affected me the same way that it affected Rachel. I was touched, humbled, and started to believe that perhaps I had found my calling after all.

Time travel and the possibilities of a second chance have always fascinated me. It was a joy to weave these concepts into the fabric of an endless love story. The words found their own way.

I am an incurable romantic—perhaps you have figured that out already. I so want to believe in a love that is timeless, a love that will always prevail.

Writing this story was like sharing a dream. Thank you for our time together.

From my heart to yours,
JL Witterick
jlw@witterickbooks.com

Acknowledgements:

This novel is a work of fiction.

Any and all references made to persons, organizations, places, events are merely the result of my imagination.

There are four exceptions:

The first is with regards to the timing of Nikkei puts and credit default swaps. My inspiration came from Prem Watsa, a man I greatly admire and had the privilege of working with during the 1980s.

The second is that references made to the benefits of a plant-based diet were cited from the documentary *The Game Changers*. This film, both insightful and relevant, made a lasting impression on me.

The third is that Muggsy Bogues is a real person and every bit as amazing as I describe him to be. He defied the odds and holds the record for being the shortest player in the NBA. Inspired by his determination and passion, I wanted to include his story in mine.

The last, but by no means the least important, is a heartfelt thank-you to my son. At the age of six, he made me a beaded bracelet for Mother's Day.

Ideas and discussion points for your book club:
(Spoiler alert)

Tom Waites knows what will happen in the future and warns Bruce so he can save Rachel. Did this story make you think about what you would do if you could go back in time?

When Bruce returns to the past, he falls in love with Rachel again—just as he did the first time. Is it possible that we are inherently drawn to certain traits and, as a result, would be attracted to the same person in another life?

This story suggests that Rachel was meant to be with Bruce. Do you believe that we have a soul mate or is it all random?

Rachel never stops loving Bruce even when she is married to Jack. If she doesn't act upon her desires, is she still being disloyal?

Rachel says that she has known Jack longer yet feels closer to Bruce. Why do you think she has a stronger bond with Bruce than with Jack?

The turning point for Jack is when he realizes that Rachel loves Bruce. At that moment, Jack turns away from her emotionally and physically. This change in Jack sets him up to see Katherine differently when he meets her in the next scene. Do you understand and forgive Jack for being attracted to Katherine and for having the affair?

Bruce asks whether it is wrong to let a million people die to save the person you love. What are your thoughts on this moral dilemma? What would you do?

Jack is a good person as evidenced by how he stands up for Bruce with the coach. The decline in his character, however, is evidenced by how he treats Bruce on their visit as well as by how easily he lies to Rachel. Do you think circumstances can make good people do bad things?

Did you anticipate the twist in the story? Were there clues that Tom Waites and Bruce Meyer were the same person? One hint is that Tom Waites finds jasmine tea soothing and Bruce comments on how he finds this beverage delightful.

The characters in this story are shaped by their childhood. General Emmerson is ruthless because of an abusive father. Bruce Meyer is strong and independent because he grew up in foster homes. Kelvin St. Clair is successful because he had to work hard to support his mother and siblings. Do you agree that we are a product of our childhood?

Bruce decides to walk away from saving the world. Yet, he would gladly die for Rachel in an instant. Is it true that love can make you selfish and unselfish at the same time?

There is much reference to fate in this story. Rachel asks the question, "Why were Bruce and I so arrogant as to believe we could alter destiny?" Do you think, as she does, that our lives are predetermined?

At the end of the novel, Bruce concludes that all our accomplishments are transitory and that love is the only thing that matters. Would you share that view?